THE TYRE

THE TYRE

C. J. DUBOIS & E. C. HUNTLEY

THISTLE
PUBLISHING

This first edition published in 2018 by:

Thistle Publishing
36 Great Smith Street
London
SW1P 3BU

www.thistlepublishing.co.uk

Chapter 1
A Gift from the Gods

On the road to Kerala, between Radapakkam and Puttur, a man stooped to pick up dead wood. The asphalt smoked, the dust burnt like hot ashes but he felt no discomfort. He was often to be found there, moving barefoot along the rubbish-strewn verges, his *vesti* rolled up over his scrawny thighs, beads of sweat on his dark forehead. All day long, he rooted about in the tangled mass of thorny bushes which bordered the ditch.

His throat dry, he panted, the noxious smoke from the vehicles attacking him like a vicious insect biting his nostrils. He squatted on his heels there at the side of the road, and spat. His empty eyes bloodshot, he gazed around, registering his surroundings as little more than fraying threads of colour, which twisted and vanished in the traffic roar. He was tired and it would have been good to linger there for a moment, but he resisted the temptation. There was work to do; a family to be fed. He gathered up his bundle of branches, shrugged it into place on the curve of his back, and resumed his arduous wandering.

He found some bits of palm, twisted sticks, relics from the last monsoon, so deeply embedded in the prickly bushes that no other collector would bother with them. But Ranji braved the sharp thorns, preferring scratches on his flesh to more rips in what was left of his shirt. His arms seemed tattooed with countless lacerations, but he did not complain, neither feeling the pain any longer, nor shirking from showing these signs of the harshness of his work. Just as the leper waves his stump to seek charity, so Ranji displayed these scars to push up the buying price of his wood. And from time to time, it earned him a reward: a few *naye paise* more than expected.

Trucks roared past, horns blaring; buses swerved perilously close, the drivers hurling abuse. But Ranji took no notice. His itchy, watering eyes were fixed on the ground. Darting here and there they inspected the dried laterite, cracked like the skin of an elephant. His calloused feet, hardened like the hooves of cattle, crushed sharp tree thorns, oblivious to their tiny stabbing needles. Poverty, and daily pain could be tamed, particularly if it were fed by the hope of reincarnation. Ranji knew and accepted his karma, and so he bent down and searched, to fulfil his destiny in this life. He picked up fragments of darkened wood, and his rough hands snapped them into smaller pieces.

He had scoured the roadside close to his home so many times that there was little left for him to collect, and so he was forced ever further afield in hope of richer pickings. That day found him further than ever from home, five kilometres at least, straying into territory which he knew was claimed by the wood gatherers from Patakgar. But no matter. If he had to confront them, he would. He had a family to support, a family that depended on his foraging. They lived close by the road, under the hanging roots of a banyan fig tree, similar to the one which had once sheltered Buddha, in a *kheti* covered with palm branches and plastic bags. It was always the highlight of his day when, bent under his load, Ranji returned there in the shade of evening.

But that glorious moment was still some time away. And so for now he batted away the flies attracted by his sweat, as he walked, half-suffocated by the exhaust fumes, and deafened by the tuk-tuks, the buses, the trucks, with the heat rising relentlessly from the asphalt. He scrutinized the dense tangle of undergrowth, which lined the cultivated fields, along which he progressed, occasionally darting in to retrieve a piece of wood that had caught his practiced eye. At times he became entangled, like an insect in a cobweb, unable to gain purchase with the length of steel which he wielded as a machete.

He noted that the big piece was still there. Last time, when he attempted to retrieve it, it had been engulfed by termites. Not much of it would be left soon, unless he could succeed in reaching it. But was it worth expending his flagging energy for this prize? In heat such as this, any movement, any effort, must be weighed against the reward it would bring in return.

He decided against it and continued his search. When he found a piece of newly-fallen wood, he estimated its worth at a glance before crouching down. By scratching the bark, observing the colour and the texture, the wood gave up all its secrets: was it good only for burning, or was it, in fact, a piece of precious wood? By the smell he identified sandalwood; by its dark brown colour, rosewood; by the texture of its grain, padouk. In those cases his face would brighten: he knew who he could sell it to and for how much. Used for marquetry he could see it in the inlay of a rich man's table. A good find!

More often though it was only fit for burning. Not much value, but of value nevertheless. When you have nothing or next to nothing, everything has a value. Wood burns better than dried dung, and gives off more heat. So the wood was sold while his wife Meena burnt dung herself at home.

Whether disappointed or delighted by his find, his soul still yearned to escape. Once in a while he allowed himself to squat down on his heels and dream. A bird would appear in the sky, and his mind would fly off with it, searching to understand the omen, because down here on earth everything had an explanation. A tortured branch in a tree reflects a cry of pain. The heavy flight of a peacock reminds us that beauty is just the mask of suffering. The song of a bird tells that anyone can be happy no matter how tiny, insignificant and vulnerable. Nature teaches her lessons; listening to her can be enough of an education. And as his dark face grew brighter he smiled up to the sky.

Just then, just above his head, a peacock landed on the branch of a margosa tree. What a marvellous sight as it stretched its legs out towards the branch. How wonderful it was to see the sparkling colours of its tail feathers, to hear its wings flapping, the sound sweet and clear above the roar of the traffic! Surely worthy to be the divine chariot of the goddess Saraswati! And it had chosen to make a stop above him – poor insignificant him! As if in a sign of friendship, the peacock curved its gracious neck towards him. Lit by a ray of sunshine, the long green feathers glittered with mother-of-pearl. Entranced, Ranji's dreams transcended his body, and his soul joined the land of the gods. How could this not be seen as a lucky omen? And where had this bird come from? Peacocks sometimes come close to humans but it had been a long time since Ranji had seen one in this area. Ranji surmised the bird must have come from the garden of the Rajah, from the vast lawns around his palace, spoken of in awe by the village people as a foreign country.

Ranji felt reassured by the bird's presence, as if it were some kind of providential sign that had been sent to him directly by a power far beyond his comprehension. He shifted his weight back onto his haunches, closed his eyes and allowed himself a moment to dream. Could it perhaps have something to do with Santosh? Santosh, his beloved son, the one in whom all his hopes resided. He had received no news from him for so long, such a very, very long time. So could this be a sign? Was this an inkling that all was well, that he was making his way in the world, far away in the big city? He looked up at the magnificent bird again and allowed a smile to play across his lips.

He returned to his task, his heart now full of certainty. He broke the wood into pieces with his machete and sorted them by length. Creating bundles with a twist of hay, he assessed the value of each. He was barely literate but not at all bad at this kind of calculation. He knew for certain that an absolute minimum of 50 rupees per day was essential for his survival, to feed his family, to safeguard the education of his daughter Surya. Twenty rupees a day were needed for the school bus alone, and then some more to make acceptable offerings to the gods. And then more besides – the notebooks, pencils, let alone the infamous, mandatory pale blue school uniform.

If only he owned that bicycle of his dreams! He could take his adored daughter to school himself, with her seated on the frame in front of him, *salwar kamiz* flying in the wind, her shining hair streaming back and whipping against his face, encircled in the embrace of his dark, scratch-covered arms. Pedalling furiously past the shuffling crowds, he would have worn a broad grin as he saved a fortune on bus fares.

A wonderful dream, but alas, likely to remain one! Where was he going to find twelve hundred rupees when he could barely manage to feed his family?

Life before had been better, far better than this. But Ranji did not complain. It was not in his nature to do so and anyway what would be the point? He considered himself lucky to be able to forage along this no man's land beside the road without too much interference from anyone else. His only regret was that he was still unable to purchase the bicycle that could change his life. Although there was once a time when he had been close to reaching his goal. So close.

His mind travelled back to that dreadful day. He relived that moment when the big black Ambassador car slowed down and stopped on the opposite side of the road. How his sense of unease had grown as five men, dressed in battle-grey trousers and spotless white shirts, got out of the car. One of them, orange turban on his head and a file under his arm, wore dark-tinted sunglasses, the same as the ones worn by politicians on election posters. Without any doubt, he was a Sikh and the head of the group. The others followed after him, seeming to approve his every word with nodding of heads.

None of them took any notice of the *harijan* who stared at them from the other side of the road. But his eyes did not leave them. And not only because of a natural curiosity. Alerted by the fall of a dead bat the previous day he had been on his guard, vigilant. It was a bad omen. Blending into the background, he observed the actions of the men dressed in their battle-grey trousers. He realised that they were employees of the state of Tamil Nadu. And he did not have a good feeling about it.

In those days, although Ranji had known that the trees along the road were owned by the state, nobody had ever come and forbidden him to pick the fruits. Now Ranji watched as the men in the spotless white shirts inspected every tree along the road: the tamarinds, the tambours, the cashew-nuts, those very same trees which were his one and only source of income. They stopped to discuss something in Hindi, then one of the men took out a hammer and fixed a notice to a mature tamarind; meanwhile, another man made notes in a notebook. They seemed to focus exclusively on the fruit, nut and spice trees, the trees that bore produce, and they didn't miss a single one. No need to be well-educated to understand what was happening here: the state of Tamil Nadu was exerting its authority. The trees belonged to Tamil Nadu, and it was taking over Ranji's livelihood.

They finally stopped at the tall hedge surrounding the Rajah Mokhtar's property. The Rajah's land extended several kilometres each side of the interstate road. Almost every crop of value was cultivated there: sugar cane, peanuts, arrack, coconut, cashews, sesame, castor oil and wheat, not to mention several more hectares of rice, peas and lentils. The Rajah's land provided work for labourers from all three of the villages around. The only enclave not belonging to the Rajah was a vast area of clay, full of pot-holes and exploited by Ashok, the brick maker, Ranji's nearest neighbour, occasionally a friend, usually a foe: the bane of Ranji's life.

And now these men with their smart white shirts and battle-grey trousers could mean nothing good. Ranji could make up to one hundred rupees a day by selling the spices and fruits. The arrival of the black Ambassador car signalled the end of a way of life for Ranji and his wife. That same day, he went to Vishnu's temple to perform *puja*, offered garlands of flowers and *pasham*, the sweet buttery flavoured paste, the delight of the gods, and implored them to save his daily bread. But it seemed that neither his prayers nor his offerings were enough to convince them.

A few weeks later, some other men with tins of paint stepped down from a truck. They made incisions in the bark of the trees and painted yellow squares and big black figures to replace the notices. When that was done, the Sikh who had supervised the operation walked over to Ranji and addressed the untouchable imperiously:

"You can no longer pick the fruits from these trees! If you do so, I will see to it that you are thrown into Radapakkam Jail."

The situation was hopeless. It was clear that Ranji would have to find another way of earning a living. But what could he do? There were no jobs for an untouchable such as him, and he was too proud to beg. Picking up sticks at the side of the road would not earn him much, but if he worked hard enough he might just make enough to keep his family from starving. Now, in addition to the wood gathering, which brought only a little money, the couple managed three times a year to get work planting rice and collecting crops in the fields of the Rajah. During those times in the year, their daily income doubled although they paid the price in exhaustion. But at least it allowed for the purchase of a sari, or the replacement of a damaged jar.

The skinniness of his legs belied the fact that Ranji was a strong and plucky man. But even so there was a limit to the number of bundles of wood he could carry on his back, and so at the end of a hard day he would have to leave some of them where they were and return for them another time. To keep the wood safe he hid the bundles behind the wild lantanas which lined the road, on the other side of the ditch, where it was almost impossible to spot them. Lots of people passed along this asphalt band, moth-eaten as an old woollen garment: pedestrians, motorcycles, tuk-tuks, carts pulled by zebu, buses, unsteady trucks overloaded with hidden travellers. So many of them that for Ranji they barely registered.

This was why, that evening, as the light of day faded, he took no notice of the red truck approaching – the Ashok Leyland, with its unstable load hidden by a large banner beseeching the goddess Lakshmi for protection. Bent under his huge bundle and heading for home, his eyes were fixed on the ground in front of him.

But, as the truck passed, he heard a strange noise behind him, similar to that produced by a rubber ball falling, but louder. Then a soft rolling and a gentle hiss, like someone stepping onto sand. Then, nothing other than the rough hacking cough of a truck in the distance. Intrigued, he put down his load, looked behind him and approached the ditch. And there, in the trench, lay a big black circular object which most certainly had not been there before!

A large tyre, brand new, labelled with a yellow and blue band and half covered with plastic film, had fallen from the truck. It was huge and of a very impressive diameter! Squatting down beside it Ranji waited for the truck to return. Maybe he would be rewarded with the gift of a few rupees for guarding it. It seemed impossible that someone could lose such a thing and not notice it.

And so Ranji waited as the darkness gathered around him. Buses passed less frequently and gradually the roar of the traffic subsided. The realisation came to him slowly: the red truck would not return, the tyre had been abandoned. An astonishing thought followed: the tyre was now like the wood, it belonged to him as he was the one who found it!

Then, Ranji noticed the moon. It was in the waxing phase, the eleventh day to be precise, the day of *Ekadashi* when widows should fast and when good fortune is said to visit those of purity of mind. Could this be the day his luck would change?

CHAPTER 2
A POOR MAN'S RICHES

D ressed in her faded, now almost colourless sari, and squatting on her heels beside the three stones that served as a hearth, Meena blew gently on the embers to re-ignite the fire. She was heating the milk from their cow with cardamom pods to make a *kheer*. And as a puff of acrid smoke rose slowly through the hanging banyan roots, Meena frowned: barely half a bucket, half a gallon, today! Their ancient cow was drying up. The sky, hazy with the dust thrown up by the incessant stream of traffic was turning a delicate shade of purple. Night would fall swiftly and with it perhaps a little let-up in the noise of the traffic. The Radapakkam road became a long snakelike procession of fireflies, casting intermittent flares on their surroundings, like a lighthouse out at sea. And in the light cast by these fleeting rays, Ranji's wife watched the bubbles form in her old earthenware pot. Neither giving birth to two children nor a life of poverty had coarsened the delicacy of her features. Her perfectly shaped full lips and beautiful smile confounded attempts to determine her age. Despite the harshness of her living conditions and being in her thirties, no lines yet showed on the smooth skin of her forehead, adorned with a yellow mark. She was preoccupied, but her concerns were not visible on her youthful face. In her ears were small silver hoops. Two narrow twisted bangles, a gift from her mother, encircled her ankles. These small things were her whole fortune.

The child Surya lay inside the hut, under a single bare light bulb dangling from its cord. Stretched out on her stomach, resting on her elbows, nose almost touching the book in which she was writing, her concentration was fierce as she attempted to trace the marks that linked the characters. Meena, full of admiration, did not disturb her. From time to time, she glanced through the gap in the wall that served as a door. She was so proud of her little treasure! Meena herself would have had no idea how to interpret the pretty arabesques of the Tamil script created by her daughter's pen. Surya, a studious pupil, had also begun to learn English, the foreign language spoken by the educated people, of which Meena knew barely a few words. She regretted not being able to offer the child a better place to study than the dirt floor, but for now she was resigned to it: this seemed to be the will of the gods.

And once Surya had finished her elementary education, and could read, write and count, the girl would be able to find a job and earn good money. And she would avoid ever being at the mercy of the administrative officials who could remove the livelihoods of the poor, seemingly at a whim.

To inspire Surya, Meena called upon Ganesh and Parvati, the deities of knowledge and devotion, and every month she scrimped and saved to ensure she could make offerings of at least five rupees out of the twenty or thirty that Ranji allocated and entrusted to her for food. And while she was at the temple, she also prayed for Santosh, of course, her eldest child, as much loved as he was missed.

Both she and Ranji felt bad about what had happened to him. He too had been a good pupil; not just a good pupil, an excellent pupil, so his teacher had told them. He might have achieved great things; he might even have gone on to a college education. There were opportunities at all sorts of institutions these days, even for *harijans*, that's what the teacher said. But it was not to be. The Tamil Nadu state and its officials had seen to that. That awful day when the black Ambassador car had pulled up on the Radapakkam Road, that day when the officious man in a turban had got out and started nailing signs to the trees – that was the day that had sealed Santosh's fate. The loss of Ranji's livelihood had reduced them in an instant from poverty to penury. In that one terrible moment, it was clear that Santosh's schooling must end. The memory of that evening when they told him he would have to put his books aside was still a dagger that pierced their very souls.

Santosh was devastated. They knew that. But he was mature enough not to let it show. He was an intelligent young man. He could read and write. All was not lost. There had to be some kind of future for him. Ranji had hoped that Ashok, the local brick maker, might find a job for him. A while ago, Ashok had bought from the Rajah Mokhtar the concession for that area of red earth alongside the road, not far from Ranji and Meena's *kheti*. Here, he employed a small gang of men to dig the clay from the earth which was then fired into bricks in the kilns in his factory. Ashok was a well-to-do man and his business was growing, but Ranji's pleas to give his son a job had fallen on deaf ears. In Ashok's eyes, Ranji was a nobody – and Ranji had never forgiven him for the disdain with which he had been treated.

But Meena saw things a little differently. Because although Ashok hadn't offered her son work in his own factory, he had recommended him for a job in the city of Thanjavur. And so he had been hired in a warehouse for building materials. What was it that he did exactly? Neither she nor Ranji knew. Santosh had left several months before and they had heard nothing from him since. The silhouette of her son waving from the bus, in his long-sleeved shirt bought specially for the occasion, was imprinted indelibly on her mind. She allowed herself the luxury of taking the memory out and cherishing it for a few moments every day. They had all smiled to make it seem like a happy scene, but Meena knew that for herself the smile had covered a breaking heart. Thinking about it now, she could feel the ready tears bead in the corner of her dark eyes.

Of course, it would have been much better to keep Santosh near them, but Meena felt Ranji was wrong to feel such animosity towards Ashok for this. Besides, Ashok's brick kilns consumed large amounts of wood and so when Ranji took to picking up sticks from the roadside, Ashok became one of his most important customers. Ranji always complained that he drove a very hard bargain and never paid a fair price, but Meena felt that on balance, he had been a good friend to them. Indeed, when she had gone to see him in secret to thank him, Ashok had been especially agreeable. He had even promised to be a little more generous in his transactions with her husband.

That very morning, with Surya at school and Ranji away, busy collecting wood, Meena had set off on foot to the village to buy some coconut oil.

She had stopped to chat to Indra, Ashok's cousin, who lived in a house near the well, when Ashok himself passed by on his cart loaded with bricks, pulled by a bullock. He came to a halt beside the two women and called out to Meena:

"Hey! My pretty, where are you going with your jar?"

"To the village," Meena replied, flattered by the compliment from such a wealthy man.

"Can I offer you a lift? I am making a delivery there," he suggested.

Meena saw the bad in no-one. It was not in her nature. She did not have a suspicious bone in her body. So she accepted the invitation to climb up and sit on the bench next to Ashok, with no thought that this might give rise to gossip.

After a few exchanges of small talk, Ashok turned suddenly to look directly at Meena and at that moment his shining eyes spoke volumes. His lips quivered as if he had a fever, but they spoke no word. Though his silence expressed his meaning more clearly than his mouth could ever have done.

After that, he turned towards her many times trying to catch her eye, but she steadfastly looked the other way, needing to avoid his insistent gaze which now made her feel so ill at ease. What exactly could he want from her? For Meena knew she had experienced this before – it brought back to her those times long ago when, as a much younger woman, her eyes would be caught by the gaze of some man, weighing up her worth like a goat at the market. She recognised that she was desired by this man, but curiously, felt nothing at the boldness of the compliment.

Ashok was a rich man. His teeth were white and the two at the front of his mouth were set with gold which sparkled when he smiled. He was not handsome: he had a big belly, but with his thick moustache and his deep dark eyes, he had a certain charisma. No, he was not handsome, but his head was well shaped, and the tone of his voice, his manner of speaking to Meena, meant she was far from insensible to him.

Meena pulled the hem of her sari forward over her face to hide her feelings – she had no wish for Ashok to see the extent of her unease. They exchanged no more words during the rest of the journey, which seemed an eternity to Meena. Her mind beset by many troubling questions, she concentrated hard, staring at the chipped polish on her toes, a rare luxury left over from the last festival, several months before. She asked Ashok to drop her off some time before they reached the market. He looked down at her with that same look of open desire that had her so confused. She thanked him briefly.

"Meena, I can take you there," he said, his voice hesitant but imploring.

"Thank you. But I can go by myself."

"You wouldn't need to carry your heavy jar."

"I am used to it," responded Meena, and set off at a steady pace towards the market without a backwards glance at Ashok.

The pretty swaying of her sari accompanied her steps.

So now Meena prepared the rice and awaited Ranji's return. Her mind wandered as she stirred the wooden spoon in the rice, augmented by green pepper, fenugreek and curry leaves. The dish was now hot and bubbling at its centre. She loved Ranji. Her man was brave and she knew he loved her, so she did not know why the lift from Ashok had thrown her mind into such turmoil.

She knew well the brick-maker's reputation as a seducer and feared that she had been thoughtless to have accepted his invitation. She must surely have been seen riding on the oxcart. There would have been talk at the well. And now the dish was cooked. Surya closed her notebook and looked up. Meena continued to stir but her thoughts were elsewhere. Surely Ranji must return soon! And what possible reason could cause a rich man like Ashok to be interested in a poor untouchable like her?

When Ranji had still not returned before complete darkness, Meena grew really concerned. She imagined the worst. Her thoughts flew to that day long ago when, her stomach twisting in anxiety, she had finally been allowed to meet the man her parents had chosen for her to marry. At just fourteen, she was little more than half the age of this man Ranji! Dread mixed with excitement, she sought the eyes of the stranger from behind the veil that hid her face. This man who would sleep with her, would make love to her and would give her children! Anxiety multiplied! But what a surprise when she realised she had seen him before! He had caught her eye when he had arrived one morning, looking for a job, with a stick on his shoulders, a bundle containing all his meagre possessions hanging from it. She had found his face pleasing. And he had been hired but he was sent to work in a distant part of the estate and she had not seen him again. And now he was to be her husband! He had been kind and seemed so very gentle. His glance at her had evoked the flight of a butterfly, hesitating to land on a flower. She realised he was also nervous of her! And his face still pleased her: she had found him handsome with his angular face that told of hard work and toil. Meena's parents, who worked in the fields, had sweated blood to afford her dowry: a cow and a goat. They had sold five animals, half their herd, to pay for the festivities. But even without these and the three musicians that accompanied them to the temple, Ranji told her later, he would have wanted to marry her anyway, he was already so in love with her. If called upon, he would have given up his liver or his spleen for her, as some resigned themselves to do in cases of extreme need. Ranji had nothing to offer but his kindness and himself. But that was more than enough for her. He did not talk much, he rarely complained. He thought a lot and meditated. He prayed. He was a good Hindu, and a faithful husband ... but now he should be there because Surya was hungry and the rice was ready!

Surya ate her rice and the spicy chickpeas that accompanied it with no particular enjoyment. And still Ranji did not come. Meena toasted a wheat pancake and dipped it in the leftovers. She lit a stick of sandalwood to repel mosquitoes, and turned off the light bulb that hung like a solitary fruit from the wire. Surya soon fell asleep lying on the mat. Meena too lay down on the much repaired *charpoi* but knew she would not close her eyes until her man was safely home. What could have kept him? Why was he not here now? Was he lying injured on the road somewhere? When, oh when would he return?

CHAPTER 3
DOUBTS AND UNCERTAINTIES

A growing awareness of the change in his fortunes had entered Ranji's mind slowly, but once lodged there it was swiftly followed by a deluge of unanswerable questions. The tyre had come to him and so was his! But what could he do with this heavy, cumbersome thing? It had some value, of that he was sure. But how much could he sell it for? Ranji knew well the cost of a portion of grilled lentils, he knew the asking price for a chicken, even knew what one should pay for a bamboo cage to keep one in, but the price for a tyre like this? The right price for a brand new tyre like this? He had no idea. And how could he take it back home? How could he hide it from thieves? Who should he speak to about it? His head buzzed with questions! Finally, he made a decision: he would roll it deep into some thorny bushes, so difficult to get into that they were certainly his best insurance against theft.

The tyre safely hidden, the untouchable went onwards as the last light of the day disappeared, his back bent under his heavy load. He followed the edge of the road, where the bitumen fell away, to get the benefit of the car headlights. He knew he was running the risk of being clipped by a vehicle, or worse, but he had learnt to leap aside when a horn sounded. Car horns and sirens reminded him that the smaller must give way to the bigger, the weaker to the stronger. That is the only absolute rule of safety. Step away from danger, step down in front of a higher caste – you negligible entity. The *dalit* was born *harijan*, untouchable, at the lowest level of the hierarchy. And with no rancour he accepted his social status, trying hard to gain, by his own merit, reincarnation into a higher caste – as a *shudra*, for instance, or even better as a *vaishya*, the caste of traders who had other people to do the work, while they sat relaxing in their shops, counting the money. But in this lifetime he jumped aside when he needed to.

One day, a taxi had caught the end of the branches in his bundle, sending Ranji into a spin as it caught on a palm branch and he almost fell. Despite the risk to his life, his persistence in following the edge of the road, was to avoid another more dangerous threat. At night snakes left the termites' nests in which they hid during the day. Eyes fixed on the ground, Ranji could detect their presence in the intermittent illumination of the headlights.

When he got nearer to those conical mounds, that looked like rotten trunks, he took even more care. He could tell which ones were inhabited: a rounded hole at the side and a pattern in the dust revealed the path of a snake. The cobra was out there, hunting probably. Be careful! Ranji called on Krishna, the god who dances with a snake, and on Vishnu, the god he had chosen as his protector. And so he advanced without excessive fear. The wood dug uncomfortably into his back, the rough rope rubbed his forehead, but he went on, the bundle on his shoulders looking like a *howdah* on the back of an elephant.

When he had started this line of work, he hadn't paid enough attention to the structure of his bundle. He often had to stop not just to rearrange his unwieldy load, but also because of the pain. Since that time, his technique had improved; he now built up vertically, sorting the wood properly and picking up the bundle by kneeling down on the ground. The most valuable wood and the straight pieces made the base of it and the twisted ones were put on the top. In addition, he did not take the weight of the load just with his back and hands but also with his head as the coolies did. These improvements allowed him to carry pretty much double the weight he had managed before, whilst also reducing the likelihood of an injury.

Ranji walked on, the blaring of horns all around him. The pad of coco fibres stung his forehead like palm tree thorns but also acted like a fakir's seat and he did not feel any pain. As a matter of fact, a callus had developed with time which could have made him look like a practising Muslim. And to avoid confusion he had requested a priest to paint there a red and yellow bindi as testimony to his Hinduism.

Nowadays he hardly felt the tension in his neck, just a sensation a bit like losing his balance – something that happened from time to time – a kind of vertigo. But his feeling at that precise moment was for a very different reason. His mind was completely absorbed by the huge tyre dropped as if from the sky.

Now, as he progressed towards his hut, his mind remained behind in the bush that was protecting his treasure. He didn't stop thinking about it for a moment. Should he tell Meena, the wife who answered his needs in six ways, his destiny? Meena the virtuous, the generous, the good mother to his children, so hard working and so capable of feeding them all with so little. Meena, who occasionally would agree to sing when he asked her to. Should he talk to her and risk being treated as a liar or worse: as a fantasist high on marijuana?

Meena had not slept at all and her heart leapt when she saw her husband finally approach the hut, bent double under his bundle. Later, sitting outside in the warmth of the night, Ranji transferred small handfuls of rice from the dish to his mouth. He seemed lost in his own thoughts. He had not told Meena of his find. He himself still found it almost impossible to believe. The heat and his fatigue could sometimes combine to create confusion in his head, but this time he was not a victim of their effects. This tyre was not the result of a dream, it existed! He had touched it, he had examined it, he had moved it into a thicket that he knew he could recognize amongst a thousand. He had been granted both an extraordinary gift and a huge burden at the same time. So what should he do?

Meena contemplated her exhausted husband. He had said very little since he had arrived home, leaning his burden against the trunk of the biggest root of the banyan tree, the one which he could see from the opening in the hut and could check that nothing had disturbed. He had gently stroked the neck of the cow, drunk deeply from the jug, dabbed some water on his sore forehead, then had gone inside the hut to look at Surya as she slept. Then he had sat down by the fire and taken his bowl, still without a word. Meena knew him too well not to understand that he was deeply concerned about something.

The flames of the brazier illuminated the deep lines between his eyes. His face was impassive but nevertheless betrayed his worries. Meena looked carefully at his arms, thinking perhaps that he had a new wound, but she could see nothing that might give her cause for alarm. She respected his silence. If he wanted to speak, he would do so when the time was right. But deep inside, she fretted with a new concern. Could it be that a rumour about Ashok had already reached his ears? Usually when he came back so late, it was because a chance encounter had delayed him. Sutikshan the herdsman, who often crossed his path was an infamous chatterbox! From time to time, tired of making small talk with his oxen, he offered a *beedi* to Ranji and they sat and talked idly about everything and nothing.

"Surya was awarded a candy at school today for reciting her lessons so well," Meena announced eventually, in a bid to start an innocuous conversation. He smiled, but said only:

"That is good," and then retreated again into silence.

She could not imagine what could have caused the furrows in his brow and the faraway look in his eyes. His mind seemed absorbed by something far more serious. Troubled she undoubtedly was, but she would never broach the subject of what she believed might be the cause of his silence. Meena was assailed by guilt. How she regretted now having accepted Ashok's offer! On the lookout for the slightest gesture that might betray her husband's thoughts, she awaited a comment on the rice which he was mechanically shovelling into his mouth and chewing slowly and thoughtfully.

Although plagued by his thoughts, Ranji was still reluctant to tell Meena about the tyre. But eventually he asked her a strange question:

"Do you think Surya would be able to read the writing on a tyre?"

"I have no idea," she answered, surprised though somewhat reassured. But while she hesitated as to whether to ask why he wanted to know, Ranji continued with another question that made the blood rush to her face:

"Ashok, does he have tyres on his cart?"

"Yes … I think so, yes" she replied hesitantly.

"In good condition?"

"Why are you asking me all these questions? You should know better than me. It is you who sells him the wood, isn't it?"

Ranji acknowledged this with a nod. It was of Ashok that he had thought first. Perhaps he would be able to sell the tyre to him. He could show it to him but he knew how ill at ease he felt with the man, and besides, how would be bring the tyre to him? He was not at all sure he could carry it on his back. How he hoped that Surya would be able to decipher what was written on the yellow and blue paper.

Like all of us, the *harijan* feared the unknown. In his ignorance he took comfort from routine. This manna from heaven disrupted the narrow path of his life and he had an uneasy feeling that he would be forced to do the one thing that he found the most difficult in his work: to sell! This was something he hated to do, though do it he must. How he disliked the process of finding customers, negotiating prices, convincing them to buy. But he did it because he had no choice. He would never have begged as did Dahia and Tarun, who lived in a hut not far from the small temple on the outskirts of Puttur. Tarun, who displayed his withered leg, and Dahia who, in her washed out colourless sari wandered with an outstretched hand, holding her last born in her arms. Ranji had never feared hard work, but hated to ask anyone for anything. He always chose action rather than relying on pity. But at the end of his musings he had come back to only one option: he must get Surya to identify the make of tyre and then he must sell it to Ashok.

"I found a tyre on the road. A huge brand new tyre with a yellow and blue label," Ranji finally blurted out, glancing with a fevered look towards the eyes of his wife. "I hid it in a thicket, an hour's walk away."

"Oh! What a blessing!" Meena cried out in relief.

CHAPTER 4
NOTHING COMES OF NOTHING

Puttur was not really so very far from the *kheti* of Ranji
and Meena, but the small shops made from sheet metal
which lined the road stopped well before the bridge over
the river. You would have to walk for a good hour from
their home to reach these outlying trading places, which
in the main were connected with transport: bicycle repair
shops, mechanics, tinsmiths, as well as some wholesalers
of spices and grains. And then almost another hour would
be needed to reach the centre of Puttur with its square, its
shops and its endless stream of tuk-tuks. Going the other
way, Radapakkam was more than three hours away by bus.
In fact, neither Ranji nor Meena had been there since that
day long ago when, coming from the East after being turned
out of their place in the suburbs of a faraway city by construction work, they had passed through the town. Seeking
a place to settle with their children they were delighted to
find this area of Puttur where spices and fruits seemed to be
not only abundant but free and accessible too. And so they
stayed there, a long time ago now, picking the produce from
the trees and selling them to passers-by, in this no-man's
land beside the road.

It was on this side of their hut that the fertile lands of the Rajah lay. A dense forest of neem and banyan fig trees separated them off from the area where Ranji and Meena's hut was located, on a kind of terrace of flat red earth in the shape of a bean with indications of the presence of clay, and a small area of grass which provided grazing for their cow.

By making one's way through the thorny bushes bordering the terrace one could go via a long winding path to the banks of a branch of the river. Some small homes built of mud and bricks accessible by narrow paths were scattered here and there in the countryside, without anyone really knowing if they were on the land of the Rajah Mokhtar, or on that of owners in the city who were unaware of their very existence.

It might have been thought that living in such an isolated spot would feel lonely, even dangerous, but in fact that wasn't really the case. On the other side of the wood, in a large clearing, Ashok the brick maker extracted clay from the land, and a little further away the Indian Oil petrol station functioned as a meeting point for travellers. Both of these enterprises certainly helped towards creating a not-unwelcome hustle and bustle. And although he knew the approach would cost him dear, because of the bricklayer's contemptuous attitude, Ranji's immediate thought had been to consult Ashok about the tyre. So, weighed down by his most comely sticks in a bundle on his back, he marched eastward.

Three men, their heads covered by turbans, their chests bare, were standing near the oven. Smoke escaped sporadically through the shell of the hulking brick monster, while they worked continuously to feed it, shovelling in wood at the lower level. Meanwhile, sitting at a distance, on his ever-present folding chair, under an umbrella for shade, Ashok kept a close eye on the operations.

Seeing Ranji approach, with a bundle of wood on his back, he adjusted his sunglasses more firmly on his forehead.

"I've brought you some wood," said Ranji, dropping his load in the dust that rose up to cover his bare feet.

"I didn't ask you to bring any! I already have all I need, and at a better price too," responded Ashok, his voice filled with mocking.

"You misunderstand me. It is a gift. I'm giving it to you."

"Do you need something from me?"

Ashok was *kshatriya*, from the caste of manual craftsmen and ruling officials. His default attitude to the *dalit* was to be patronizing. Since the untouchables had been granted electricity, medical care and free schooling, his overt contempt of these "privileged" people – as he called them ironically – had multiplied. Benefits should be reserved for those who desperately needed them, according to Ashok, and the *dalit*, selling his wood but paying nothing at all in taxes, went against the spirit of this rule, he believed.

That the son, being a boy, had the benefit of this new system, he could accept, but he felt differently about little Surya. He felt it was simply preposterous that this girl child, effortlessly at the top of the very same class as his own daughter, benefitted from the system too, without her father having to pay even a penny towards it. In addition to this, Ranji was married to the prettiest woman in the village, and that, as well, just didn't seem right.

It was a long time ago that he had first noticed the beauty of Meena, shining out despite the poverty of her clothes. How unjust were the gods to have condemned this beautiful woman to live under the palms of a makeshift hut! How he would have loved to take her home with him!

This foolish dream fed his aggression toward Ranji, rubbing salt into the wound. Why should Ranji have got such a prize, compared with him – he, at least, paid his taxes!

"I just came to ask you for a bit of information, only information…" said Ranji timidly, "… about your ox-cart."

Ashok pressed a finger to his sunglasses, the better to appreciate the discomfort on the face of the *dalit*. Could Meena have said something to him? But he had done nothing wrong. Dreaming of stealing the wife of one who is less than nothing cannot be considered reprehensible. It was evident that he had been far less fortunate than Ranji in the lottery of marriage. When Ashok's wife Puna smiled, her catastrophically positioned teeth resembled the twisted stems of corn after a storm, and the diamond stud in her nose reminded one of nothing more than a piece of quartz stuck into a ball of clay. And when she walked, dragging her feet, her huge belly and behind were reminiscent of a cow ready to calve. If Ashok had put in a good word for Santosh it was solely for the sake of Meena, not for this despised man.

"Aha! I knew it – so you DO want something from me," he said, his tone full of scorn. "Well, what do you want to know about my cart?"

Ranji fiddled nervously with his loincloth, summoning up the confidence to see this mission through.

"Your tyres… What kind are they?" he said at last.

"My tyres? No idea, they turn and that's good enough for me!"

"The size of the two of them? Is it the same?"

"Of course it is! What a stupid question!" the brick maker scoffed.

"Would you mind if I take a look?" asked Ranji timidly.

"Look if you want to! It's over there, behind the oven," said Ashok folding his glasses and stretching out his legs which had grown stiff from sitting down for so long. Then, casting another glance at the pile of wood dumped there by Ranji, he changed his mind.

"Hang on a minute. Why are you asking?"

"I am looking into something ..."

"Are you planning to buy a cart?"

Ashok knew that Ranji already struggled to feed his family, so by what miracle could he find enough money to make such a purchase? Unless... unless this errant scoundrel might be hiding the real reason for his visit with this tall tale, designed specifically to throw him off the scent. Maybe it WAS something to do with Meena! But he couldn't for the life of him figure out what it could be!

"Can you afford to buy yourself a bullock to pull the cart? Or would you get your cow to pull it?" he continued with a sneer.

"How Ashok's tone has softened because of his curiosity," thought Ranji, sensing some hint of weakness hidden in the mockery. This perception gave him the courage to push his advantage.

"For the moment I am just looking into it. You can read, can't you? Can you tell me what is written on the side of your tyres?"

"Aha, I see. So this is why you gave me that wood. You HAVE given it to me, haven't you? You won't turn up tomorrow asking for payment?" Ashok retorted.

"It was you who told me that every favour has a price, wasn't it? I ask only that you read me what is marked on the tyres of your cart."

"Go, go! I'll come with you!"

Half an hour later, Ranji left clutching a piece of paper with some sketchily drawn numbers and letters none of which he nor Ashok really understood the sense of.

"They are references," the bricklayer had claimed. His
curiosity had been piqued and he was now desperate to find
out what Ranji was planning to do with this information.

"I am just looking into something ..." repeated the *dalit*
when pressed.

With a smile on his lips, Ranji resumed his wood collecting, now with a lighter heart. He had taken a big step
forward and was pleased that, at just the right moment, he
had remembered Ashok's own rejoinder from the first time
he had gone to sell him wood: "He who gives nothing gets
nothing." He had left that time without wood and without
money, but for his second offering, Ashok had given him a
small amount of money straight away. He didn't regret his
investment this time either, but now he would have to work
hard to build up another bundle and get home before dark
with his goods.

He hoped that Surya would not be asleep and that she
would be able to read to him the words written down on his
paper. He was pretty sure that the new tyre was much larger
than those on Ashok's cart. He really needed to go back to
see it to remind himself of its size. And if Ashok didn't want
it, it would find another buyer he was sure.

"BRIDGESTONE 185x60Rx17.5," Surya deciphered
the letters on the paper, "and below: GOOD YEAR
195x60Rx17.5."

"Are you sure?" Ranji asked, frowning. "Is it not the same
thing written on both of them?"

Surya reread them aloud, following the characters with
her finger.

"Yes *bahba*, that is definitely what is written."

"So that proves that you can drive with two different
tyres," announced Ranji.

"But the numbers are very similar," Surya pointed out. "Maybe it is the name of the manufacturer which is different."

"Ah yes! That must be it, I do adore you, my little princess," said Ranji, moved by the cleverness of his beloved daughter.

"Tell me *bahba*, when will Santosh come home?"

"I don't know Surya. He is working a long way away and to travel home is expensive. But he will come back to see us as soon as he can, I'm sure."

"Why hasn't he written to us?" asked Surya sadly.

How Ranji would have loved to have the answer to that question! He had resisted the temptation to ask Ashok about Santosh for fear that the question would reveal how worried he was. He had no desire to appear anxious in front of that man. But Ashok might have known something. A few days after Santosh had left, when passing the *kheti* the brick maker had stopped his cart specially to tell Meena that their son had arrived and that his employer seemed satisfied with his recruitment. But since then, no letter had arrived from Thanjavur to confirm these words of Ashok.

Ranji had faith in his son but he was concerned about him. He knew that the boy was resourceful but he was concerned lest his youth and inexperience were exploited. Scared that, if forced to sleep on the street like so many young people, he might fall into the hands of dacoits. He knew that Meena was even more troubled and was waiting for some communication with growing impatience. Despite all that, he had not yet allowed himself to spend the three hundred rupees required for transport to find out for himself – the money so patiently set aside and hoarded for the purchase of his bicycle.

And so, he took refuge in prayer and in interpreting signs and omens. This recent cooperative attitude of Ashok must be a favourable sign. Santosh was fine. If he had not yet written to tell them so, it was because his work didn't allow him the time. Ranji must remain calm, trust in fate and a letter would arrive.

CHAPTER 5

THANJAVUR

Santosh had made a huge effort to appear happy and confident on that momentous day all those months ago when he had waved goodbye to his family, but in reality it was a very different story. With the tiny knapsack on his back containing the few items Meena had packed for him, he was full of trepidation as he climbed aboard the bus which was to take him towards the East. He was leaving behind his family, his friends, his school, the place where he grew up – everything he had ever known. This was a decisive break with his past and he was heading into an uncertain future. The image of his parents and of his little sister, standing on the roadside, waving, his mother determinedly holding back her tears, stayed etched on his mind long after his departure.

The preparations had started a few weeks earlier when Meena had decided that her son could not present himself as an educated man at a job interview in the only formal clothes he possessed. Although his trousers had been kept exclusively for school they were now tight everywhere and so short that they barely reached his ankles. His shirt too had faded to a nondescript colour and was missing several buttons. It had been fine for school but was definitely not suitable for a job in the big city. So, taking one of their last remaining banknotes from the old Pepsi can, she took her boy to the tailor in Puttur. The only time she had been to this shop before was to order Surya's pale blue school uniform, and she remembered that the man had been courteous to her. But although she knew it was in the handicraft quarter she couldn't remember exactly where it was. A man smoking a hookah in front of his textile shop, pointed them in the right direction and she found her way through the crowds to arrive at the tiny shop, no bigger than the *kheti*.

The tailor, an elderly man, was sitting on an old iron chair, behind a Singer sewing machine from the days of the British Raj. He lifted his glasses to get a better look at the kind of customer he was dealing with, while Meena, anticipating his likely reaction, hastened to explain that Santosh needed a new, but inexpensive, set of clothes. To assure him of her ability to pay, she produced the banknote and stood holding it awkwardly in front of her.

The old man got to his feet with difficulty and started to take measurements with the tape-measure he had hanging around his neck. Having scribbled them down on a crumpled piece of paper he produced several rolls of textile from his cheapest range. Finally, after a long negotiation about the price, a delivery time of one week was given and accepted by Meena.

Another banknote, carefully put aside in the Pepsi can to go towards the purchase of the bicycle, had been taken out and given to Santosh before he set off. And so, a hundred rupees in his pocket, he had taken a succession of different modes of transport to get to Thanjavur. After the journey to Puttur, another blue and yellow bus took him to Radapakkam, from where a third bus deposited him at Tiruchirappalli station. There, he squeezed into the third class compartment of the train from Chennai which, after multiple stops, brought him to Thanjavur station, which was just another short bus ride from the very centre of the city.

And so he found himself alone, at seventeen, in a big city for the very first time in his life. He had learnt in school that Thanjavur was the ancient capital of the kingdom of Chola and he now looked up in wonder at the ornately carved pyramid of the temple of Brihadeeswarar, capped by its great granite dome, which dominated the centre of the town. All around him, the place was teeming with life. There were crowds of pilgrims, shoppers, hawkers, beggars – even white-skinned tourists with their cameras constantly at the ready. He watched one group as they followed a lady guide dressed in what looked to Santosh like a man's uniform. No tourist had ever been seen in Radapakkam, let alone in Puttur. They seemed to take photographs of everything – roadside stalls, tuk-tuks, children, even a zebu grazing peacefully on the lower branches of a *neem* tree. What was it that they found so extraordinary about these things? Santosh wondered. But a more important question nagged at him too: how on earth was he going to find *Srivati and Co*?

He realised he had absolutely no idea of how to go about finding his destination. All he had was the name of the company written on the piece of paper that Ashok Kapoor had given him, and also a name – Nadar – who he understood to be the boss who hired labourers for the warehouse where the construction materials were stored. This information would certainly have been enough to find somewhere in Radapakkam, but here the seemingly insurmountable scale of the task ahead of him made his stomach churn with a feeling that had little to do with his need for food. The *pani-puri* which his mother had so fondly prepared for him had not gone very far to assuage his appetite, and hunger was now added to his woes.

Santosh bought something to eat from a street vendor, and asked the man for help. The man admitted he had no idea where this company *Srivati* might be, but he was kind enough to hail another street seller and ask him. This one did not know either and advised Santosh that most of the big businesses in Thanjavur were either mills or foundries, which made him start to worry. Finally, a flower seller suggested that it might very well be in the Ramasamy Pillai district, the industrial area that ran alongside the banks of the Cauvery River.

As he had no better idea for finding the place, Santosh heeded his suggestion and pushed his way onto a bus that he hoped was going the right way. The architecture of the streets and the incessant coming and going of tuk-tuks reminded him of what he had seen of Radapakkam, but Thanjavur seemed to be built on a completely different scale. The bus took an age grinding its way through the traffic of the city centre before turning onto a road that ran alongside the river. At this point, a number of his fellow passengers got off and Santosh was finally able to find a seat at the back next to a respectably dressed middle-aged man. As he looked approachable, Santosh checked with him that he was indeed going in the right direction.

Fate must have been smiling on him. This man not only knew of the *Srivati* company, but he also took an immediate interest in this young man who had travelled from so far away to seek work. The man turned out to be a pastor of the Lutheran Mission of Thanjavur – which had been established in the eighteenth century, he explained to Santosh with considerable pride. On realising that Santosh knew neither the city nor anyone there, he offered to put him up temporarily, at least for a night or two. Astonished at this unexpected kindness, Santosh had no idea how to express his gratitude sufficiently. The man introduced himself as Akhil Amaguri and wrote down his name and address in a faded notebook which he took from his pocket. He ripped out the page and offered it to Santosh, before jumping off at the next stop. Santosh touched his hands to his forehead in a sincere gesture of gratitude.

"Help a poor man, and God will reward you," the man replied, getting to his feet with a kindly smile.

Following Mr Amaguri's directions, Santosh got off the bus at the stop just before the end of the line, where he found himself in the middle of a road clogged with heavy traffic. Malodorous smoke hung in the air, making the sky dusty and the large number of trucks pumping out choking exhaust fumes told him that this must be the industrial area. He passed a few buildings topped by billboards and posters written in English. That one must be a mill, he deduced from the rolls of silk stacked high on a cart. There was a dry cleaners identifiable by the smell of ammonia. Further on he came to a foundry, then another, but still no sign of *Srivati and Co.* He walked on for maybe a kilometre before finding anyone he could ask. At last he spotted someone: a taxi driver was waiting there, sitting behind the wheel, in front of a new building on which fluttered a foreign flag.

Without moving or even altering his grumpy expression, the man grunted that he should take the third street on the left and then the second turning on the right. Santosh thanked him and kept on walking. His feet, used to walking barefoot, were uncomfortably hot in his new shoes. It was Ranji who had insisted on him having these. He had said it was important to seem worthy of getting a job in the town, and without shoes, how would Santosh impress this man Nadar whose name was repeated in the hut with the same reverence and respect that was usually reserved for prayers to Shiva? So they had dipped once again into the money carefully hoarded in the can of Pepsi, now dramatically depleted, to buy him some smart shoes, and as the XL was the only size on special offer, he had ended up with vastly oversized shoes in which his feet slipped around uncomfortably.

At last he came to a high-walled compound with a sign above the gate, proclaiming *Srivati and Co. Building Materials.* His heart leapt. But when he entered the bustling courtyard and weaved his way past the stacks of palettes and piles of bricks and heaps of sand, to reach the office at the back, Santosh received an unpleasant surprise. During his long journey, he had given free rein to his imagination and had often pictured the warm welcome he would receive on his arrival, as the famous Nadar read over Ashok's weighty recommendation, nodding his head and smiling. He hadn't thought for a moment that there would be any competition for the job. But when he enquired of a man leaning against the back of a truck and smoking a beedi, he discovered that he was not the only applicant at *Srivati and Co* that day.

In fact, there were at least twenty men of all ages lined up in the shade of an awning at the side of the building. At the front of the queue, a narrow staircase led up to a room on the first floor closed off by a glass door. Feeling extremely apprehensive, he joined the end of the line. Until that very moment, the possibility that he might not actually be hired had not occurred to him, but now, seeing the number and the average age of the other candidates, he had a painful twinge in the lower abdomen and a strong desire to pee. None of the men in front of him was carrying a backpack, which presumably meant they all lived in the town. In addition, he must surely be one of the youngest. Was it possible that his father had been tricked into getting involved in a hopeless venture? Knowing the animosity that existed between Ranji and Ashok, the notion that he himself might now be the victim of this rancour completed his feeling of demoralisation. Crushed by this thought and suddenly exhausted, his legs began to tremble. No longer able to hold back, he dropped his backpack and rushed to a distant corner to relieve himself behind a pile of scrap metal, praying that this misdemeanour would not be observed and jeopardise further his chances. As he re-joined the queue, an older man, dressed similarly to his father in a grubby *dhoti*, came out through the glass door, head down, apparently knowing that he had not been hired. But then the young man standing in front of Santosh in the queue turned to him. Although a bit taller than him, he couldn't have been much older. He smiled in a friendly way.

"Where have you come from?" he asked Santosh, visibly intrigued as much by the bundle he carried as by his oversized shoes.

"From Puttur."

"Where is that?"

"Far away. Very far."

"My name is Abihrup, I am from Rajakrishnapuram. What about you?"

"I am Santosh."

Rajakrishnapuram: the name meant nothing to Santosh, but he guessed it couldn't be far away, as the young man had no luggage. He checked his assumption with his new acquaintance.

"No, I've also come from a long way away, but I have an uncle who lives here. That's why I have applied. Have you worked for a construction company before?"

"No. I have just left school. My family did not have much money. But I have a recommendation…"

"From what I have heard, they are going to take on five of us," Abihrup said softly, leaning toward Santosh.

"So we definitely have a chance then," Santosh whispered back, as much to convince himself as the other young man.

Abihrup was a handsome young man, his cheekbones strong and prominent though marked by a few blemishes, and dark hair as shiny as his eyes, with a friendly face and a manner to match.

"Don't you have any luggage with you?" Santosh asked.

"I left it at my uncle's place in Ramasamy Pillai Nagar. It's not far from here. I really hope they take me on."

"It would be great if they took both of us," Santosh responded.

The line inched slowly forward. Abihrup remarked to his new friend that almost everyone standing in the line seemed to be older than them. Just then though, another youngish man came out making a V sign for Victory with two fingers. Anxiety gave way to a new hope: could it be that his youth would appeal to the recruiter?

Two new contenders came to lengthen the line before it was Abihrup's turn to climb the ten steps that rose to the glass door. Santosh wished him good luck and they shook hands. This interview lasted longer than the previous one and when his new friend came out, a broad grin was plastered on his face. Then, instead of leaving like the others without a word or a look, he came right up close to Santosh and whispered a few words in his ear. "The guy is very direct. He wants strong young men, able to work in a team. Now it's your turn. Good luck, my friend."

The time had come for him to climb the stairs and face his future. Santosh took a deep breath and his father's story of the officials and the episode of the Ambassador car came back to him. The incident had left a big impression. In order to earn money and perhaps one day have that same kind of power, he knew he would have to work hard and honour the gods. He took his courage in both hands and introduced himself spontaneously to the man who opened the door. But he was only the doorman.

He followed the fellow along a corridor. Behind the glass walls he could see some people busily sorting through paperwork and others speaking self-importantly on the telephone. He suddenly felt small and insignificant, miserable. Why on earth had he ever thought Mr Nadar might be interested in employing him – an untouchable from a humble roadside shack?

The doorman indicated a solid door on which Santosh read: Mr J Paniandy. Santosh knocked discreetly and on being summoned inside he found himself in a rather small office, facing a big man with a very dark complexion wearing rimless glasses. On his desk a rotary fan whistled like a kettle and, as the flow was directed at the gentleman, it caused a dark lock on his forehead to flutter. Mr Paniandy stared for what seemed a very long time at Santosh, with the intensity of a horse dealer studying a young stallion's teeth, then, with a gesture, he ordered him to sit down on the chair opposite him.

"So, tell me your name, your age, where you are from and what you are able to do?"

Santosh had practised for this during his trip, imagining that it would be exactly these questions that he would be asked. He had expected to be interviewed by Mr Nadar, the boss of this company, but apparently it was this Mr Paniandy who was in charge of recruitment.

He explained the situation of his family, his schooling, and added that he knew how bricks were made – which made Mr Paniandy smile slightly – and emphasised his willingness to work hard for a serious company like *Srivati and Co*, which he knew to have a most excellent reputation. He spoke from the heart, mentioning his knowledge of English, and confirming that he had studied physics and even knew how to solve equations with up to two unknowns.

This last point caused Mr Paniandy to arch his eyebrows, while an amused smile played on his lips. Until that moment his face had given very little away, although his hand had scribbled furiously in a notebook as Santosh had spoken, and in fact he had wondered if Mr Paniandy really was listening or if he was doing something else entirely.

"You are very young, but you speak well. That's good," he said, fixing his gaze on Santosh.

This gentleman was looking an untouchable in the eyes! Santosh, instead of breaking the gaze, sustained it, because now he felt a glimmer of hope.

"So you can read and count."

"And also speak English, sir!"

"Speaking English too ... 15 rupees per hour, 9 hours a day, 6 days out of 7, paid at the end of the week. That's my offer boy!"

"To do what, sir?" Santosh dared to ask.

"The preparation of orders. We are the largest depot of builders' materials in the region. Iron girders, concrete blocks, bricks, wood, cement ... You will work under the direction of Anand who will train you. A word of warning! Any delay, the slightest mistake, you're fired. Does that suit you?"

"When should I start?"

"Tomorrow. Be here at seven."

Trying to control his excitement, Santosh rose, and bowing with a *Namaste* gesture that he repeated three times, he clasped his hands to his chest, and thanked Mr Paniandy sincerely for the trust placed in him.

Paniandy opened his desk drawer and pulled out a wad of small green cards striped with yellow. He took one from the wad and in a rectangle that had been left white under *Srivati and Co*, he wrote *Santosh Firtavel* and pointed to another rectangle:

"You need to get four photographs. You should stick one here and give the other three to me tomorrow morning when you arrive."

"Of course Paniandy *sahib!* Tomorrow morning at seven – I'll be here!"

His heart was soaring as he walked back out through the glass door and looked down from the top of the stairs at the others still waiting hopefully in the line. He had already done the rapid calculation in his head and had worked out that he would be earning the princely sum of 810 rupees per week! He could hardly believe his luck.

He lingered in the yard for a while, watching the comings and goings, imagining himself preparing the pallets of bricks, counting bags of cement. But soon the issue of where he was to live came back to him, and with it the realisation that he had absolutely no idea what it might cost. Another imponderable question! But meanwhile he knew he must find a photography store, and so he returned to the centre of the city on the same number bus that had brought him there. He paid a fortune for four rather average quality images, realizing with some alarm how incredibly expensive everything was in this town. He was left with only thirty rupees.

Arriving at a crossroads where a group of *tuk-tuks* were waiting for customers, he asked how much it would cost to go to Mr Amaguri's address. For the equivalent of one hour of his new work, he could be taken to the *Tank District*. Too expensive! he said. Another driver suggested that he could perhaps ride with another passenger if one turned up who wanted to go in the same direction, and then he would be able to share the costs. But he would have to wait. Now that he had the photos and the promise of a job, he was happy to do so, and blend into this mass of patient people who, from their impassive expressions, seemed to spend much of their lives standing around waiting.

He sat down on the pavement, put his bundle beside him and took out the employment card given to him by Mr Paniandy. How proud he felt to see his face there in the white rectangle beside the name of the company. He could hardly believe he had been given this miraculous opportunity. Tomorrow he would show up at the entrance and nobody would know that two days earlier he had been sleeping on the ground in a hut beneath a banyan tree three hundred miles away.

It was now around 6pm, the end of the working day, and as the offices had closed, the swell of people leaving and the dance of the buses and rickshaws intensified. A couple asked to go to the *Tank* and agreed, as was customary, to share the fare with Santosh. During the whole journey, the lady's eyes kept returning to the young man, lingering on his bundle, his shoes, noting his appearance of poverty. But as for him, he looked around him in wonder. He stared at the houses, the different businesses, seeking to familiarise himself with this city that was to become his own. When the driver stopped near Gandhiji Road and pointed out a narrow street as his destination, Santosh offered the 5 rupees that was his share, but the lady insisted he should pay nothing. He thanked her with his most appealing smile. Without a doubt the people here were really friendly! He had a good feeling that Thanjavur would suit him very well and he didn't care how hard he might have to work.

A lopsided sign at the corner of the street indicated that this was indeed the location of the CF Schwartz Mission. Santosh turned into the street, certainly more peaceful and less crowded than those downtown. The road was lined with two-storey houses. Soon he was standing outside a white building with barred windows that had the appearance of a school. He went in through an open door, and found himself in a dark hallway that opened onto a courtyard from which he could hear children's voices.

A girl in a *salwar*, who seemed to be about his age, came towards him. She wore a Christian cross over her long white shirt. He introduced himself and asked to see the pastor.

"You need to go upstairs," she said, whilst another girl with a shoulder bag, joined them and explained to him: "This is the school here."

And so half an hour later, Santosh found himself eating a chapati stuffed with chickpeas and peppers in the private apartment of the Pastor Amaguri and his wife Suzanna, along with three other young people who were also sharing their meal. He felt the situation was almost unreal: he had been in the city less than twelve hours but already the hut beneath the banyan tree seemed like a strange mirage from another distant life. How could he ever have imagined that things would work out so well, so quickly?

At the end of the meal, the Pastor kindly suggested that Santosh should stay with them for a while, to give him the chance to find alternative accommodation, and he also suggested that he could ask his congregation if anyone had a spare room. Santosh was so grateful that he wondered aloud why the Pastor would accept to host a homeless untouchable such as himself. Mr Amaguri gave him his answer:

"Have you ever heard of Thiruvalluvar's moral code?" he asked,

"No, sir. Who is he?"

"Oh, he passed away many many years ago, probably close to two thousand years, but he left us his wisdom in a long poem called the Tirukkural. According to him every human being deserves to be accorded the same rights, not just the wealthy but the poor too. It is the duty of the former to assist the latter. What we are doing is only following that simple rule, and I am sure you will do the same in the future when you discover that there are always poorer people than yourself.

"He was a good man," said Santosh, "And you are a good man too. Could I buy that book?"

"Probably you could. But it is hard to read and, to be honest, quite boring! If you are interested in reading, my boy, read anything and everything which might be useful for your job."

"Thanks so much *sahib ji*, thank you so much for everything."

That night he wrote a letter to his parents telling them of his good fortune. He read and re-read it several times before slipping it into an envelope. But he became troubled as he pictured the scene back at the *kheti*. The image of his mother lifting down a jar of water perched on her head seemed pitiful. He saw in his mind's eye the figure of his father laying down his burden, his arms streaked with blood, dust rising around his feet as he entered the hut. He heard again the incessant murmur of traffic and the noise of the car horns that woke him in the night.

In that moment, he realized that nothing he had written could seem believable to them, even though it was the complete truth. Despite their worst fears, he had met no obstacles in his way. Nobody had tried to take advantage of his inexperience. In fact, he had encountered only friendship, trust and kindness. And in the space of just a few hours, he had found a job as well as a safe and comfortable place to stay. But how could he describe all this to his family left behind in penury? He tore up the letter and resolved to write another time.

Chapter 6
A Fortuitous Meeting

In a gesture of munificence, the government of Tamil Nadu had made an electoral promise to provide the people of the area with a well, and provide a well they eventually did. Though it has to be said it took four years for this promise to come to fruition; and even then, a certain reluctance to squander too much money on a handful of poor peasants meant that the pump eventually provided was operated by hand. It was certainly less tiring to use than hauling up a bucket on the end of a rope, but the design meant that it could have only one user at a time. As a result there was always a small crowd gathered at the well, as much out of necessity as for the pleasure of socialising.

In the countryside, and often in the towns too, it was the women who assumed this chore from an early age. This task had the dual merit of not only giving them time together away from the menfolk, but also of strengthening and toning their necks. From this duty they developed an upright bearing, coupled with a natural grace and elegance that needed no artifice to embellish it. So, dressed like the paupers that they were, they made their way along the roads and paths, carrying the heavy jars on their heads but usually laughing in good humour.

Now there were eight of them at the well, women who had come on foot from their huts, happy just to be together and gathered round the well ready to exchange the latest gossip. Combining their daily chores with a bit of fun, they amused themselves like children, splashing each other as they waited for their turn. They knew they might as well get some pleasure while they carried out their everyday tasks.

The water flowed into the plastic cans and the iron jars that shone like jewels in the sun. While pushing down on the pump handle, Indra, the cousin of Ashok told risqué stories, related to her generous curves, revealed now by her wet clothes. The others laughed while they waited. The water sprayed, tinkling into the containers with a sweet sound.

Meena had three containers: one would go on her head, the other two would hang from her arms. She had put in its place the small pad, the crown of the poor, which adorns the top of the head. She would lift up there a pitcher full to the brim, weighing over fifteen kilos. This accessory adorned the hair of a peasant from adolescence. The ritual lent itself to conversation at the well and many unlikely tales were aired: it paved the way to the sharing of confidences as well as to gossip and salacious tales. Ah, if the men had only known what was said about them!

When Indra described the amorous advances of her husband the night before and her attempts to refuse him, peals of laughter rang out. Suggestions were rife on the thousand and one ways to get what one wants from a man. They were all united in one opinion: men are unreliable, manipulated at will and totally incapable of doing two things at one time! Theirs was undoubtedly the weaker sex! But even so some harsh words were reserved for their own sisters, and no-one held back from openly teasing the prettiest of the group about their supposed clandestine love affairs.

Meena was not entirely at ease. She knew that she was being observed, and she waited for the barbed comment. She had seen the pointed look Indra directed at her as she talked about the marital difficulties of her cousin who apparently didn't knead only the clay, and Meena feared Indra making a very direct reference to their intimacy on the journey to the village. She smiled at the jokes, but remained on her guard. She listened but said nothing that could attract attention, and maybe jeers, towards herself. Bahmini, the wife of Vicash, a good friend of Ranji's approached her:

"Have you heard anything from your son?" she asked Meena.

"No. Still nothing."

Bahmini sympathized but had little idea what to add. She knew that her son, younger than Santosh, might well have to go too, one day. Separation, silence: it must be hard for a mother.

"You should go to the post office at Puttur," intervened Indra who had joined them and heard their conversation. "They may have mislaid a letter," she said, helping Bahmini balance the load on Meena's head.

A lost letter? Well, lost or not, Meena had never to that day received any letter. And why would anyone send a letter to someone that could not read anyway? But maybe one addressed to Surya? She latched onto and then clung to this idea. Could she be so bold as to go to the post office to find out? When she got back from the well, why should she not take the bus to Puttur? What if, by chance, Indra could be right? They might not even know that the family existed! It was certainly a possibility. And now that this possibility had occurred to her, she felt she must know, and as soon as possible. And to find out would cost her only the 15 rupees for the bus journey to Puttur.

❧ ❧ ❧

Far from there, Ranji continued with his own activities under the cover of the coppice. He was trying to cut up a large dead branch of jackfruit which had fallen in the last gale. He wielded the machete with little need to look at what he was doing while his mind remained in the thicket where he had hidden his treasure.

The night before he had woken with a start from a nightmare, sweating profusely: Someone had stolen his tyre! He pictured the thorny bush where he had left it. He remembered pulling leaf-covered branches into position all around it so it would not be seen from the road. But did he take enough care? What if a curious passer-by, familiar with that place, had noticed the unusual shape? But remembering the heavy weight of the tyre gave him some comfort – it wouldn't be easy to move. Then his mind wandered as he started to wonder about the strange black colour of tyres in general. He wondered about the factory that used the sap of the rubber trees that grew in the mountains. Resin that was not black but a milky white. By what magic did this white material become black? How much work would it be to collect all that resin? How much would someone pay for all that resin transformed into black? So many unanswerable questions!

One thing though he did know: he absolutely must bring the tyre back to the hut. He would not sleep soundly until his treasure was at his home, safe from others' avarice, for he was sure that if someone else came across this marvellous brand new object, then it would be stolen. There was no way he could tell anyone, not even his friend Vicash. It was a shame as he could have asked him to transport it on his cart, but he feared that Vicash might be talkative. Better not to share this miraculous news. The only solution was to roll it at night, hiding as soon as he heard the sound of a tuk-tuk. It would take time.

Ranji had collected five bundles of wood which he had put down at the foot of the flame tree. He crossed paths with Ram, a *dalit* like him, who, with his team, was starting to plough the Rajah's rice field. They exchanged a few words. A fleeting thought to ask him for help quickly disappeared as he feared that he too could not be trusted to keep the matter to himself. Ranji continued on his way, looking for wood and step by step he made his way closer to the thorny bush where his gift from the gods was hidden.

His machete needed sharpening. This put him in mind of the incident of the dented wing. Two years earlier, he had witnessed a bad collision, near the bridge, between a car and a cow crossing the road. The driver was injured, his eyebrow badly split, blood streaming from the cut. But kneeling down, instead of bemoaning his own fate, he apologised to the animal. While a crowd gathered around the dying cow and the wounded driver, Ranji had spotted the wing of the car – this had been thrown off to the side and no-one else had noticed it. An ambulance had been called and while all the bystanders stood around commenting on the scene, he had surreptitiously pushed the piece of metal into the ditch with his foot, with the idea that he could do something with it later on.

The situation turned out well for Ranji, as well as for the blacksmith of the village. In exchange for this large piece of dented wing, he had made for Ranji three knife blades and this machete cut from sheet metal.

Since that transaction, without actively willing them to happen, Ranji had watched out for accidents and did his best to recover the fragments of iron and plastic that resulted from them. Sometimes when a piece was useful, the ironworker gave him one or two or even five rupees. Other times Ranji kept them for his own use to make a hook, or to strengthen the structure of his hut, to plug a hole, or to fix a utensil. The misfortune of reckless drivers supplied his toolbox. Tonight he would make sure he used a stone to sharpen his blade. And as always, his mind would take him back to the memory of that flap of bloody flesh hanging down over the eye of the careless driver, and he would give thanks to Shiva.

When Ranji reached the hiding place, it was already dusk: the sky was turning red before the twilight, with that purplish hue that seems to thicken the air and envelop the fields, flattening their vivid colours. He found, with no difficulty, the pile of dry spiny plants and quills that he had taken care to pile up on top of the tyre, and he was pleased to see that it really was impossible to imagine that anything could be buried under there. He waited for the sun to set behind the mountains before he removed the things piled on top.

It was then that he noticed, for the first time, the deep parallel stripes similar to lines of writing that adorned the tread, and the small rubber spikes protruding from the sides of the tyre like nipples on the belly of a pig. He had seen nothing like that on Ashok's cart!

With both hands he turned the enormous tyre until he could see the yellow and blue label and then took out the piece of paper from his pocket. There was certainly a resemblance to the marks that Surya had deciphered, but nothing was exactly the same. Instead of BRIDGE-STONE there were other letters. He must note them down, but how? A brainwave! He picked up a thorn and scratched into the skin of his thigh big signs that made up the name APOLLO, followed by different numbers.

He stayed there for a long while sitting thoughtfully, his back to the road, in order to hide the object from passers-by, and breathed in that peculiar smell of rubber. What life might this tyre have known had it stayed on the truck? What kind of vehicle was it intended for? Maybe a bus, or perhaps a large truck. Certainly not the cart of a brick maker! Maybe intended for a rich entrepreneur from Radapakkam or even Thanjavur, rolling on from city to city, crushing dung and snakes with no mercy! And today perhaps it would have arrived at the depot where Santosh was! But instead, it had chosen to stop off near his home. How strange was fate!

Then as the sun sank rapidly down below the hedges, the first crickets awoke, the day became night and the bats, that seemed to practically skim his turban, began their incomprehensible ballet. The roar of trucks and cars, and their headlights, filled the space. It was time to go.

Before picking up his bundle of wood, Ranji decided he would bring the tyre one step closer to his *kheti* by rolling it to the next thicket. Walking bent under the weight of his burden, he lost himself in his thoughts. In this way he avoided dwelling on the discomfort from his load. If he did not find a buyer for the tyre, he could still offer it to the shop adjacent to that of the blacksmith. The shopkeeper had stacks of tyres piled up. Certainly they were no longer of any use as tyres, but he gave them a second life. By cutting into them and fashioning handles, he made them into extremely strong baskets which could be used to transport sand and cement on construction sites.

That would be the very last resort and a terrible shame to see a brand new tyre of this size finish up as a basket to carry mortar without having ever traversed any tarmac! Obviously, the price he could ask would be much less interesting too. But his quandary was this: how on earth was he to find potential buyers if he didn't tell anyone about his discovery?

The figures of four men passed by on the other side of the road, silhouetted by the light. One, twisted like the branch of a cashew tree, passed by limping, the second dragged his right leg behind, moving his neck like a wader in a pond. The other two, bent over with fatigue, were speaking Hindi, he realised. That night it seemed that all the night wanderers carried sticks and this made Ranji wary. As his family was leaving Chennai they had come across similar bands of nomads. Often thieves, and sometimes violent, the very poor would attack those less poor than themselves.

Lurking in a thicket, Ranji waited until they had gone far out of sight before he emerged with his tyre again and started to roll it along like a hoop. He had tried out this method on the previous evening and had set himself the goal of going beyond the giant termite hill.

The insects built these tall tapering edifices at night, building up soil and twigs from the ground. By day the structure looked like a small abandoned mausoleum, but in the darkness and silence of the night you could hear a hissing and feel the presence of a multitude at work.

Alerted by a warning hoot, Ranji hid himself in the shadows at the side of the road and used the opportunity to catch his breath. The moist air announced a change in the weather, possibly a thunderstorm. Suddenly he felt something cold and light slithering over his foot. He feared he knew instantly what it was: cold, smooth, and not so far from the termite mound. He froze, not moving an inch, holding his breath. He invoked the blue goddess. It was possible it could just be a harmless snake, but it could just as likely be a cobra whose bite could take his life within hours.

Ranji was familiar with the terrible habit of the cobra of hiding in termite mounds. An oval hole in the side indicated that one was present and it was clear that the mound nearby must have been host to one recently that he had not noticed before. When he could no longer feel the sensation of the serpent on his foot, Ranji moved on with infinite caution, annoyed at not being able to hide his tyre in that place. Reptiles are home-loving and they love warm, quiet places. Ranji had noted that his tyre retained heat and stayed warm long after the sun had set. Dreading to find the reptile coiled inside, he had taken extreme care and handled it like a precious object. Fortunately, the snake seemed less observant than himself. Perhaps he was naturally wary of this hiding place which would, after all, have been alien to his normal habits.

He finally reached the place he had intended to stop, and between bursts of headlights and horns, Ranji attempted to push the tyre on even a little further. He just needed to go straight on for a good long distance, then take the next turn in the road and the banyan tree would be in sight. Maybe three nights more and the treasure could finally be at home. He was anxious to show it to Meena. He knew she would be worried because he was so late. She would not say anything of the sort, but he would read it in her eyes. Meena's eyes spoke louder than her words.

Ranji loved his wife more than anything. He intended to keep his promise, made for better or worse, that he would make her happy. When she saw the tyre, he knew she too would understand that it could change their lives. If he were able to sell it for two thousand rupees, for example, he could buy not only the bicycle but other things too: a gold embroidered sari for Meena, perhaps a stove with a gas bottle, and lots of books for Surya. He was just about to carefully hide his tyre again when suddenly from behind him he heard a voice:

"Where are you going with that, my friend?"

Ranji gasped. The voice coming from the shadows was sweet as *kunja laddu*. A man, naked and emaciated, was advancing towards him under the pale light of the moon, his body covered with ash. His long silver beard hung down like the roots of a fig tree. A high bun crowned his head. The *sadhu* stopped, leaned on his staff and asked:

"What are you doing with that tyre risking your life in this way on the road?"

Releasing his grip on the tyre, the *dalit* joined his hands and bowed to show his respect for the holy man:

"I found it, *babu*, and I am taking it home with me."

"You didn't find it! It came to you. Bhagavati is rewarding you for doing *puja* by sending you the wheel of the sacred chariot," the *sadhu* said, crouching down near the tyre. "Let me see it! Do you have a match?"

Ranji did not have a match, but the headlights of a vehicle remedied that. Quite impossible to guess the age of this man who seemed to see as well as a young man. In the beam of light, Ranji had time only to glimpse the coloured marks on the forehead of the hermit, but a quick glance at the side of the tyre seemed to be enough for him.

"Aha! This is a premium tyre my friend. It's an Apollo Acelere, I believe. This is the kind of tyre you find on public works vehicles, sometimes on trucks."

Ranji's eyes widened in astonishment.

"How do you know this *babu*?" he asked, quite taken aback.

Again engulfed by the darkness, the sage took his time to reply. His past belonged to the past, he had not referred to it for so long that he was reluctant to explain now. He finally decided that he would:

"I have not always been a *sadhu* my friend. In the past, I was an engineer. And in the course of my work I had to learn a lot about tyres!"

"Ah!" was all that Ranji could manage! His surprise was total. He had absolutely no idea what to say as he absorbed this extraordinary piece of information. The situation was too unusual not to see in it a new sign of destiny.

"Well then, it is the gods that have sent you," he said, overwhelmed by a wave of gratitude. Suddenly more prosaic, he added, "How much might it be worth, a tyre like this?"

"Money! Money is not bad, but money has no importance my friend."

"Maybe not for you, *babu*, as you receive offerings, but for a poor *harijan* like me, money means the survival of my family!"

"Well then, I would say five thousand rupees minimum if you had to buy it," the *sadhu* ventured.

"Five thousand rupees!" Ranji gasped. "Are you sure?"

"I said if you had to buy it! I do not think this is your case, is it?"

"Oh no, of course not! It is selling it that I need to do now," Ranji confirmed.

This estimate, well above what Ranji had imagined, emboldened his heart. Nearly three times more than he had thought in the best case scenario. Although he still needed to find a way to sell it, once he had achieved this he should have more than enough money to buy not only his bicycle but so much else besides. The treats that would be made possible by this sale rushed headlong into his mind: a journey to Thanjavur for the whole family, long trousers with a belt and a white shirt for him, a gold embroidered sari for Meena, books for Surya, a curved saw, a second cow, goats even ...

"Five thousand rupees!" Again he tried to imagine this amount in bank notes. A fortune!

"Hey, hey, don't dream too much my friend!"

The scrawny figure rose, outlined by the brightness of the moon, and started to speak:

"Do not believe, my friend, that doing without material things is any obstacle to joy! My pleasure to have met you is great, and yet I possess even less than you! The wisdom of Buddha led him to encourage his followers to walk without thinking about anything, as you did until today, letting your mind wander and simply enjoying the pleasure of having good legs to walk upon. I see your excitement at the prospect of being able to afford possessions. But what you do not see, because you are already imagining how the sale of the tyre can change your life, is that this could be the start of problems for you. You will be afraid that it will be stolen. You will strive constantly to find a buyer, you will feel acrimony and disillusionment. Until now you were content with your life, but now your contentment will be overturned and upset. Maybe one day you will regret having stumbled upon this heavy lump of rubber!"

Ranji was struggling to absorb this speech when the *sadhu* continued: "And remember: this is a high-end tyre, enhanced with silicone. You will struggle to find a buyer, unless you have acquaintances in the army. They use these for their big trucks."

A solution, the army! He had seen those huge trucks trundle by on their massive tyres, just as elephants plodded by on legs thick as tree trunks. Of course the warnings of the *sadhu* were full of common sense, but the holy man would never be able to understand how useful a bicycle could be to him. And not only for him but good also for the welfare of his whole family.

"How can I thank you for your knowledge, good man?" said Ranji, desperately seeking for a coin in a fold of his *vesti*.

"Have you had dinner?" he said at last, finding nothing else to offer.

"Thank you. I only eat when I need to."

"Would you accept a roof for the night? My place is simple but if you accept, I would very willingly offer you our *charpoi*. Its strings need repairing but you would be under a roof and on a more comfortable bed than the ground," offered Ranji, desperate to find a way to thank the *sadhu*.

"A roof? Why would I need a roof? See what a beautiful place he who shelters us has provided, and with so many stars! Isn't it enough? And is a bed useful to one who has abandoned his worldly pleasures and who lives only for the spirit? On the other hand, if you have fresh water, I would drink with pleasure, my water bottle is empty."

"Then please come with me! My *kheti* is only half an hour's walk away."

"I'll be happy to walk there with you."

"First, I must hide my five thousand rupees."

"Do not dream so much, my friend. Don't dream!" admonished the holy man.

On the road to Radapakkam, two shadows suspended between heaven and earth advanced towards Ranji's hut. One, paying heed to his five bundles, swayed dangerously, resembling a young elephant. The other, chanting mantras through his thick beard, looked like a scarecrow. Head tilted down towards the harsh land, Ranji was careful where he put each foot and concentrated hard. Meanwhile, that of the *sadhu*, detached from what was happening around him, appeared to rise up in the night to the starry sky.

CHAPTER 7
THE LETTER

A t the door of the small post office in Puttur, twenty people were queuing under the sun waiting their turn to go
inside. Meena had not told Ranji of her decision to come here.
That morning when she had returned from the well, she could
not get Indra's suggestion out of her mind. Should she go to
the post office to check if perhaps a letter had been lost? A
completely unforeseen and unique experience. When living
in a country where one in four men and one in two women
were illiterate, the postal service was completely unknown to
most of them. The post office was perceived as a kind of unat-
tainable sanctuary reserved exclusively for the educated. And
anyway what address could be given when the recipient lived in
a hut made of palms? Heart thudding at this bold step she was
making without telling her husband, she hoped desperately to
finally get some news of her son Santosh. So she had taken the
bus, found the post office, and was now waiting patiently in the
queue. Fifteen minutes later she had reached the entrance,
and now she was right on the point of taking this vital but
nonetheless terrifying step: finding out if, by any chance, a letter from Thanjavur could possibly have been mislaid.

Here inside the heat was stifling. Like hungry chick-
ens, customers were crowding against the wire netting that

protected the officials from the people. The most suffocating heat seemed to be reserved for these customers who jostled and shuffled and sighed, exhausted by their wait. So, to the surprise of Meena, the sanctuary she had imagined for the educated seemed instead more like a chicken coop. So what good was it to study if one found oneself here, packed together like poultry? This was the thought that ran round Meena's head. Everyone was talking at once. There were grumbles and complaints about the slowness of the service and of the rudeness of the staff.

Meena had a long time to wait before she spied, behind the grille, five postal workers idly chatting whilst quietly rifling through their papers. They seemed totally cut off from the hubbub all around them, insensitive to the invective of even the most aggressive customers. At the far end of the post office, half hidden behind huge stacks of files, sat a man who seemed to be the post office manager. His serious expression reflected the importance of his work. To Meena he bore a strong resemblance to the officials who had confiscated their trees: the same crisp white shirt, the khaki trousers, the same closed face. His elevated position had earned him the privilege of a circular oscillating fan which fluttered the pages of the ledgers he was perusing, while the rest of humanity around him sweated profusely.

Anguished by this first step, Meena kept a close eye on everything: a shift first to the left, then to the right, straining to see through the wall of people waiting in front of her. She hoped to be served by a staff member capable of understanding the problem, but the woman who passed the letters through a hole in the grille looked to be no more accommodating than any of the others.

Gradually, the grille was coming nearer and Meena's heartbeat quickened. Her heart was in her mouth. An altercation broke out between a customer and the woman at the counter. A letter which had not arrived. A problem of the wrong address according to the post office worker. Not true, the customer claimed. Meena trembled: this could be exactly what had happened with the long-awaited letter from Santosh. One of the officials who had been chatting came to the rescue of the counter clerk. With his gilt-framed glasses and his perfectly trimmed moustache he seemed to be the deputy. Meena was anxious to hear their conversation and pressed close against the man in front of her, little thinking that this might be a source of titillation for him. The man suddenly turned round fully to face her, with a salacious look plastered on his face. Horrified she felt his hand on her body. She grabbed at his wrist and dug her fingernails in deep.

A well-dressed gentleman who had seen what happened signalled his approval of her action. The scoundrel feigned ignorance and took his turn in front of the postmistress. Behind Meena, the queue continued to file into the office, in an orderly line, as in a temple. When Meena was finally standing in front of the counter, the female teller got up and a man came to take her place. Had this change been made because she was an untouchable? She felt even more anxious now, having prepared herself for speaking to a woman. The worker first of all started to rearrange the papers he found in front of him. His attention to the task seemed to indicate its importance and Meena dared not disturb him. After a moment, he looked up at her with a querying expression. She explained her reason for being there. This worker also had a small perfectly trimmed moustache, just like his boss, and eyes empty of any expression. He still seemed absorbed in his preferred task of shuffling papers but at least now he was listening.

"Tell me again your address," he ordered.

"On the side of the Radapakkam road, near the Rajah's property and the petrol pump."

His stare now transfixed Meena. Suddenly she felt herself to be observed by all these well-educated people who surrounded her. How could this poor woman who had nothing possibly expect to receive a letter? And what audacity to turn up there in her shabby sari!

"One moment," he said, with a look which could best be described as disdainful, and he got up to go towards a colleague.

A discussion. Hope was reborn as another person glanced toward the metal mesh, then towards a wide shelf bent under the weight of letters and packages that seemed to have been abandoned. Another discussion. The counter clerk shrugged, then looked back at Meena. She saw the other official slowly rise and walk towards the shelf.

"My colleague will have another look, stand to the side," said the counter clerk imperiously, summoning forward the next customer.

Now it was Meena's turn to be crushed against the counter but she felt nothing. Her eyes never left the worker who had grabbed the stack of post from the shelf, dropping some letters in the process, then gathered them up, all the while talking with the deputy. He picked up one from the pile, examined it, moved it to another place, then went back to the first pile. Meanwhile, at least three clients had already passed through, one to buy stamps, one to complain about a letter, one about a change of address. If all enquiries were to take this long, the line would stretch as far as her *kheti*, thought Meena. Could a letter from Santosh, so precious, be there, among all these other messages, all these envelopes, all these abandoned letters, long awaited by an anxious mother from her son, or a wife from her husband? She was sure hers was there somewhere. She felt as if, through the screen, the words surely written by Santosh were sending an inaudible signal in her direction. She fumed inwardly at the infuriating slowness with which the official reviewed each document, read the address, sometimes hesitated and then methodically added it to the stack on his right. It made her mad, but she clung to the hope of her letter finally being discovered in the pile on his left which was gradually decreasing one by one.

How long did she stand there with her eyes fixed on the postal worker's hands? Thirty minutes? One hour? Then finally she saw the man linger over a small envelope. He turned it round in his hands but did not add it to the pile on the right! He called the deputy and pointed out something to him. Meena's heart flipped when the deputy, envelope in hand, came towards her.

"The Radapakkam road. That is not enough to be delivered safely. You must tell your correspondent to be more specific next time!" he said sharply.

Meena nodded. She would have promised anything. The letter clutched in her sweaty hand, she rushed to the exit of the post office, ecstatic.

In the queue for the bus, she examined at length the rectangle of paper without understanding what was written there. She was dying to know what was in it but she hadn't dared open it. Terrified of losing the letter, she slipped it inside her *choli* between the material and her breast, feeling its presence as if her son had returned to be nourished at her breast. She retrieved it though after only a few minutes, suddenly afraid that her sweat would ruin it.

She noted with alarm that the poor quality paper had softened. Near her, a much older man, dressed like a bureaucrat, with carefully combed hair and a gold wrist watch, was reading the *Times of India*. Intrigued, he had been discretely watching Meena's actions. She saw him looking. An idea came to her: Would she dare to ask him? He didn't seem to be at all arrogant, nor seek to take advantage of his caste as did some Brahmins. The thought of now having to wait for Surya's return for the news from Santosh seemed even more unbearable to Meena than this expedition in the heat. The opportunity was too tempting, but how would he react?

A glance at the man and a charming smile, before she embarked on her mission. The letter trembled in her hands, as she held it out towards him. The man smiled back. He had understood without her having uttered a word.

"You want me to read it to you, don't you?" he enquired kindly.

"Oh, yes please *sahib!*"

"It comes from your lover?"

"No *sahib*! From my grown-up son Santosh! He works in Thanjavur."

"Ah! You are very young to have a grown-up son," replied the gentleman folding his paper.

Then he took the envelope that Meena proffered and slit it open using an arm of his glasses. All around Meena, the people pretended to ignore the scene but their ears were straining to hear. Taking out the letter, the man produced from inside it three one hundred rupee notes which he quickly put back in the envelope. He asked Meena to stand closer and began to read softly:

Thanjavur, January 14, Makar Sankranti
My dear parents, darling Surya,
I have just figured out why I have not received any news from you. I wrote two months ago, and entrusted the letter

66

*to Naresh, the driver from Birla Cement who delivers to
us. He was supposed to go to Radapakkam but he did not
make it. Another driver from Coromandel told me last week
that Naresh had been in a bad accident near Srirangam
and is dead. I understood then that he wouldn't have had
time to take my letter to you, so now I am writing another.*

*I am sure you must be worried at having no news, so I
can reassure you right away: I am fine and I like my job.
It's certainly harder work than learning in college but I am
earning money and sahib Javed Paniandy has given me a
new role because he found out that I can write pretty well
and do the accounts. To begin with I was carrying hun-
dredweight bags and iron girders. But now I help to keep
the inventory of the warehouse and of the stocks of goods for
all the construction work. I write down in a notebook what
comes in and what goes out. This is much less of a strain
and better paid too.*

*I live with two other employees of the company in a room
rented from the uncle of one of them, Abihrup. It is pretty
close to the depot, so I can walk, and the rent divided by
three still leaves me with something to live on, and means I
can save a bit too. I am sending you what I have set aside
so far. Certainly not as much as I would have liked to send!
Bahba can keep some of the money for his bicycle, but most
of all it is to continue to support Surya in her studies.*

*As it is you who will read them this letter, sweet little sis-
ter, I beg you to work hard in school. Nothing is impossible
nowadays even for the dalits, but we need to study better
and work harder than the others.*

*Thanks to my new salary, I hope one day to buy a motor-
bike so I can come to see you. But it costs a lot of money so
I must continue to save and I am sorry to say I probably
won't see you or the banyan tree anytime soon, unless there*

is the chance of a lift. I am on good terms with the delivery men but the rules are that they are not allowed to take passengers. But you never know, maybe something can be arranged.

That's all from me. I hope all three of you are healthy, that bahba does not kill himself with work, and that mum thinks of me as I think of her, at all times. I kiss your hands,
Your Santosh who loves you

The gentleman carefully folded the letter and gave it back to Meena whose eyes had become misty while listening to these sweet words. Even he seemed touched by what he had just read. "You're lucky to have such a good boy!" he said, with kindness in his voice. The people around them nodded approval of the man's words! For a brief moment Meena had the impression of being someone of importance. Later when she was sitting on the bus, squashed in next to a pregnant woman holding a basket on her lap, she was still greatly affected by Santosh's letter tucked in against her breast. She imagined him, now with a small moustache and a white shirt, shoes on his feet, notebook in his hand. How proud she was of her son! Waves of happiness washed over her, as she travelled back towards home. Her heart overflowed with an intense joy that she hadn't felt in such a long time. How glad she was that she had been inspired to follow Indra's advice!

And how happy Ranji would be too, when he heard the small voice of Surya reading the letter! She vowed to make an offering to the gods the very next day.

Having found a new hiding place for his tyre, even more secret now that he knew its real value, Ranji and the *sadhu*

had set off towards the *kheti*, the *sadhu* chanting his mantras and Ranji suffering in silence under the weight of his burden. When they finally reached the hut, Meena was still awake. Tremendously excited as she was to announce her news, she had not yet told Surya, believing that her husband should know the good news first. She saw first his skinny legs and heard the muffled sound of the wood being dumped on the ground. But he was not alone. She jumped up.

"Ranji?"

"Meena! We have a guest," Ranji said quietly to avoid waking Surya.

Meena lit the oil burner and poured water into the bronze bowl that the holy man offered to her, as he invoked Lakshmi, the goddess of wealth and beauty. He implored the wife of Vishnu to protect his hostess. And then she could resist no longer. Associating the wonderful events of that day with the presence of the *sadhu*, she presented her sweetest face to him:

"Won't you taste a bit of the *pachady*?" she suggested to the hermit, then serving a tiny piece of spicy fish to Ranji, she added quietly to him: "Today is a happy day, we have news from Santosh!"

Ranji raised a questioning eyebrow. Meena, brandishing the envelope as if it were a sacred offering whispered,

"It was given to me at the post office in Puttur. It had been mislaid. Santosh is doing well; it is written here."

She hesitated to take out the three notes, a fortune, in front of the hermit who had renounced all material possessions, but she couldn't resist the pleasure of seeing Ranji finally smile. Since the tyre had come into their life, she felt as if he was permanently worried.

"And this is a gift from Santosh," she said, showing him the money.

Ranji stared in open astonishment. Meena had said nothing to him about a trip to Puttur and now here she was, producing banknotes from an envelope and speaking of Santosh as if she could read what was written! Instead of rejoicing, he felt displeasure and frowned, finding these events suspicious. How could Santosh have come by so much money? He knew well the beauty of his wife and although he had never before suspected her of anything untoward, he was overcome by apprehension.

"You have a generous boy," the *sadhu* said, coming to the rescue of Meena who was clearly bewildered by this reaction from Ranji. "The gods have been good to you because you honour them appropriately."

"One more favour please *babu*," said Ranji grabbing the envelope and handing it to the wise man. "Could you read to me what is written there?"

"I will with pleasure!"

Once he had finished reading, the *sadhu* gave the letter to Ranji who had squatted on his heels, as usual, as he listened to the deep voice of the holy man. Gradually, as the image of his son had taken shape through the comforting words written down on paper, his former concerns and suspicion gave way to emotion. At that moment, as Ranji looked at the indecipherable script a drop fell from his eye and blurred the writing. A tear of pure joy that mixed with the ink and made a purple flower-shaped spot. Ranji's hand, holding the notes, trembled.

"Thanks for the refreshment," said the sage rising. "And now I must continue with my journey."

"Wait!" said Ranji, jumping up like a coiled spring, and, under the stunned gaze of Meena, he offered one of the three notes to the *sadhu*.

The man brought the note to his forehead in a gesture of gratitude but said:

"Vishnu's blessing be upon you and your family, you are as generous as your son, but what do you want me to do with this banknote? I need nothing, while you need everything. You offered me water and it was enough. Keep this and make good use of it."

"You could make an offering," suggested Ranji.

"You can do that yourself," said the sadhu. "*Namaste!*" And with this traditional blessing, and with folded hands, he bowed to Meena and Ranji and set off in the direction of Puttur.

"You will never get your bike if you waste money like that!" scolded Meena. "You did well to offer a gift, but you should have been more reasonable. Ten rupees would have been fine..."

"Woman, you have no idea what you are saying!"

Ranji took Meena by the hand and led her towards the dead trunk under the banyan tree that served for them as a bench. The lean silhouette of the *sadhu* had melted away into the darkness and the only light was a small flickering flame that hung on a pole in front of the hut.

"You do not know what you are saying because you do not know what the *sadhu* told me. First, think how we can barely survive a week with one hundred rupees, but he can live a month or two! He has nothing but his bowl, his grimy *dohti* and his stick, but his wisdom and especially his knowledge about tyres is immense. So, do you know what this holy man taught me about my gift from the gods? Invaluable information: the value of my tyre! And have you any idea what it's worth, this tyre? Fifty times what I wanted to give him. I did the calculation several times while we were walking: five thousand rupees, that means fifty notes of one hundred! Do you get it? Now Meena, of course you are right: he would have accepted a penny, but not such a gift. These three notes are to be shared by all three of us and are not to be set aside just to save for my bicycle. This is what I have decided: one will go in the can of Pepsi where we put the money to buy it. One is for you and for the gold embroidered sari that I know you dream of having. And with the last one you should buy an outfit for Surya, books for her studies and I will get a flashlight for when I come back in the darkness."

Meena listened carefully to the words of her husband, saying nothing. She found his words full of wisdom, and turning towards his face dimly lit by the flame, she was happy to read in it a new serenity.

"The sari will wait until you have sold it," she said, gently kissing him.

CHAPTER 8
SRIVATI & CO

On his first day in his new job, Santosh had woken before sunrise and stared around blearily at his unfamiliar surroundings. Where was he? He rubbed his eyes as the events of the previous day came into focus in his mind. Of course! This little attic room was at the top of the Amaguris' house. He smiled as he remembered his good fortune in meeting the Pastor on the bus and their kindness in welcoming him into their home. Then he splashed a little water onto his face from the pitcher in the corner of the room and steeled himself for the events of the day ahead.

It was still before six when he arrived at the bus stop nearest to the house, but the streets were already filling with workers, heads down, as they scuttled to work in the grey light of dawn. Santosh had not slept at all well, and did not feel on top form, but he was so happy that this feeling faded as soon as he set foot in the courtyard of Srivati & Co. And it vanished completely when he saw Abihrup – the young man he had stood next to in the queue for work. They hurried towards each other.

"I knew they would hire you!" exclaimed his new friend. "I am so happy for you! What are you going to be doing?"

"Preparing the orders."

"With Mr Anand? Me too!" And the two young men grinned at each other in delight.

Mr Anand was a tall, rather severe-looking man in his early fifties who reigned over the depot like an ancient sovereign and had a profound knowledge of every nook and cranny of his kingdom. He knew the precise location of the tiniest screw and washer and he could recite the product specifications, catalogue references, manufacturers' credentials, wholesale and retail prices of any item with the assurance of a learned scholar. With a beedi always smouldering between his fingers, he was famous for his uncanny awareness of the whereabouts of every one of his staff at any moment of the working day; it was said he could sense a malingerer through the thickness of two brick walls.

Santosh was to work under his eagle eye in the Department of Wholesale Materials. This involved handling a large range of products including heavy, cumbersome objects such as bags of sand and cement, steel joists, concrete posts and metal girders. These were all stored in the courtyard outside the warehouse, under the heat of the sun which was where his new friend Abi (as he liked to be called) had also been assigned to work.

As the orders came in, Mr Anand would shout out the requirements and his team of workers would have to track down the materials and stack them in bays ready to be loaded onto the delivery lorries when they arrived. At first it was difficult to remember in which part of the warehouse or courtyard the different things were stored, but Santosh soon began to discern a system and as the morning wore on, he needed less and less guidance from his supervisor and colleagues. However, he was not used to such intense physical labour and the sweat was soon pouring down his forehead and running into his eyes.

"You should tie something round your head," Abi called to him when he noticed Santosh wiping away the perspiration with the back of his hand. Santosh said nothing, but grinned in acknowledgement, while at the same time admiring the way his new friend could hoist a huge concrete block above his head with the minimum of effort.

When it was time to take a break for lunch, Santosh asked him how he had found the morning's work and Abi replied: "Oh, this is a piece of cake compared to my last job."

"And what was that?" Santosh wanted to know.

Abi told him he had been a sand diver before coming to live with his uncle here in Thanjavur.

"A sand diver?" repeated Santosh who had never heard of such an occupation.

Abi explained that it had been his job to dive into a river with an iron bucket, drag it along the river bed to fill it with sand and then bring it up to the surface where he would empty it into a barge. It had been gruelling work, requiring not just considerable physical strength but also the ability to hold your breath for minutes at a time under water.

"And so what happened?" Santosh asked him. "Why did you stop?"

"Technology!" said Abi with a rueful smile. "The man who ran the operation sold his concession to a bigger firm. They brought in a generator and a huge suction pump and that was that. All ten of us young divers were out of a job."

Santosh was impressed by his tale and wondered what he should say if he was asked to give an account of his own life story. But the opportunity didn't arise because at that moment Abi caught the eye of another young man of a similar age and sauntered over to introduce himself. His new acquaintance, Chan, was a muscular stockily built young fellow. He had a shy, diffident manner but Abi clearly had a gift for putting people at their ease, because Chan was soon giving them the benefit of the wisdom he had gained in his six months working at Srivati. Santosh listened eagerly, taking careful mental notes of everything he said. They were still deep in conversation when Mr Anand blew his whistle and barked the order for them all to return to work.

The three boys quickly became firm friends, as Santosh settled into the rhythm of his new life at Srivati & Co. He enjoyed the feeling of companionship, but under the stern gaze of Mr Anand, he was also aware that this was a competition too. A good knowledge of where everything was kept was a huge advantage and so Santosh's excellent memory meant that he was soon acknowledged as one of the quickest workers in the yard. His father used to quote a proverb to him – *Than kaiye thanakku udhavi* – the best source of help is in your own hands – and he thought of this now as he scurried hither and thither picking the orders in double quick time. However, he also came to an arrangement with Abi and Chan that they would work together and help each other out.

The strong feeling of affinity and their close working relationship forged a strong bond between the three young men and it was not long before they started to discuss the idea of sharing accommodation. Abi had been living with his uncle who would soon be leaving Thanjavur, as he worked on the railways and had recently been assigned to another station. This meant that Abi would have some spare space which he was only too happy to share with his new friends. It was a room with a kitchen and a small balcony on the top floor of a house in the Ramasamy Pillai Nagar district, only about a kilometre from their place of work. The three friends realised that the rent would be quite reasonable if they divided it between them and the proximity to Srivati would mean they could economise on bus fares too.

So when Abi told them that his uncle had left and that the room was free, Santosh prepared to tell Pastor Amaguri that he had found a new home. He had been extremely happy staying with the Amaguris. He enjoyed the caring atmosphere and the comings and goings of the orphaned and abandoned children that they took under their wing. His heart was full of gratitude to his hosts and he believed that they had grown fond of him as well. And so, on his way home that evening he stopped to buy *modakams* scented with rose, wrapped up in a copy of the *Times of India*, as a gift for Mrs Amaguri. He handed it over with effusive thanks for all their kindness and they all promised to stay in touch and share their news. As Santosh went up to bed that evening, he thought he even caught a glimpse of a tear in the eye of his kindly hostess as he bade her goodnight.

Because he took his work so seriously, Santosh had been able to learn a lot very quickly. The Department of Wholesale Materials soon held no secrets for him and without really meaning to, Santosh gradually took on a leadership role among his colleagues. They looked to him when a decision needed to be taken and continually sought his advice on where the more obscure items in the catalogue were stored. This had not gone unnoticed and Mr Anand, although not used to giving compliments freely, had taken him aside one lunchtime to express his satisfaction with Santosh's work.

In fact, Santosh was now eyeing the possibility of a move to the Tool Department, which was more technical, as well as being located inside the warehouse. The manager of this section, Mr Jaigin, who was clearly Mr Anand's right-hand man, had also become aware of Santosh's potential.

He noted with approval how, in any rare lull in the work, Santosh would go over to his section to cast his eye over the tools and machines, asking questions about their use and how they worked.

Then one morning, about three months after Santosh had started at Srivati, Mr Anand did not appear for work. His absence was not altogether surprising. For some days the old man had been coughing a lot and his eyes misted over frequently. Although famously strict, he had never been known to lose his temper, but a few days ago when one of the young apprentices had come to him for advice, he had snapped at him and sent him away with sharp words ringing in his ears, which was not at all in character.

Some days later Mr Anand had still not returned to work and Mr Jaigin seemed to be taking on many of his duties. When Santosh asked him what was going on, the manager's expression became serious. He said briefly that Anand would certainly not be back. The poor man was very sick. Meanwhile he himself would not be able to carry out the two functions indefinitely. There would very likely be a reorganization of the warehouse.

A week later, Mr Javed Paniandy, came down from his office at the end of the glass-panelled corridor. This in itself was an exceptional event. The big man paced the aisles, shaking hands with the employees. Everyone realized that something was wrong. He announced that they should all meet at noon on the dot in the Tool Department.

At the appointed time, one hundred and fifty employees were gathered together when Mr Paniandy, with a sense of the occasion, informed them of the death of Mr Anand. After more than twenty-five years' loyal service to the business, he had succumbed to pneumonia in the early hours of the previous day. Deepan Jaigin was to be his replacement, and there were to be some changes in the management structure of the company.

The next day, Santosh was eating a mango, sitting on a pallet of bricks with his two friends, when Mr Jaigin approached them.

"Santosh, would you come with me for a moment?"

His mouth full of juice, Santosh raised his dark eyes to the new warehouse manager and got up to follow him.

Mr Jaigin walked briskly ahead of him without a word. As Santosh walked to the staircase that led up to the offices, he was suddenly gripped by anxiety. Had he made a mistake on an order? Mr Paniandy had been very clear about the penalty. His concern grew when Mr Jaigin headed for the door of the director, but noticing Santosh's worried face he gave him a reassuring nod.

Javed Paniandy was sitting behind his desk, just as he had on the day of Santosh's interview, but now somewhat slumped in his chair. It seemed that his responsibilities weighed heavily on him. The fan was stirring the air, but Santosh observed that the boss must have put some gel on his hair because not a single hair was disturbed by the breeze.

Paniandy looked up at his visitors, closed the file he was studying, and motioned them to sit down:

"Santosh. So, how are you?"

"Well Paniandy *ji*. Very well in fact," answered the boy, quite surprised by his friendly tone.

"Are you happy in your work?"

"Of course *sahib!*"

"Have you had any equations with two unknowns to solve?"

"Oh no *sahib*, but I have had to search hard for the quick-setting cement!" Santosh replied without realising he was being teased. Part of the stock had been lost due to a burst pipe and it had actually been very difficult to find any to replace it.

"Poor Mr Anand should have ordered a bigger quantity," said Mr Paniandy, "but now it's Mr Jaigin who is going to be in charge of all this, isn't it Jaigin?"

"Yes Paniandy *ji*. And I'll need help ..."

"From someone intelligent, who can count and do equations for example?"

"And someone who is serious about his work," Mr Jaigin added.

Santosh felt the blood rush to his head. Were they suggesting what he thought they were suggesting? He hardly dared believe it. A smile spread across his lips.

"Do you feel capable of doing the inventory? To identify products that move quickly and those which do not sell? To help Mr Jaigin to optimize the stock?"

Santosh thought for a moment before answering. He was being offered a promotion – and he was clearly being offered a job designed for an older employee. Why him? And what would be the penalty if he was not up to it? He was also worried about how Abi and Chan would react. But his overwhelming feelings were those of pride and delight.

"It is a great honour you do me Paniandy *ji* and Mr Jaigin too," he told them. "I assure you I will put all my heart and soul into it and do my very best to justify your confidence."

"Well in that case, we will give it a go," said Mr Paniandy. "I can offer you 20 rupees per hour, but you will be on trial for a month, after which, hopefully, you will be officially appointed as assistant to Mr Jaigin. One month should be enough if I can believe what I have heard about you."

Santosh turned to Mr Jaigin and saw he was smiling broadly at him. It felt for a moment like he was the big brother he had never had. How he would have loved to have someone like him to look up to as he was growing up – someone who could teach him about cars and women and cricket and all the other mysteries and pleasures of life.

"I do not know how to thank you," Santosh said with emotion.

"Start now! We have over 1500 products here to check!"

In the hallway, Santosh thanked Mr Jaigin again. The latter confessed he had been surprised by his ability to remember everything that was said to him and by his curiosity too.

"You must have done well at school, right?"

"Yes," said Santosh. "I should have gone to Kampur Institute of Technology, but my parents were too poor."

"It's a shame. Yes, really a shame. Oh, and by the way," said Mr Jaigin and he looked Santosh directly in the eyes, "I wanted to tell you I am also a *dalit*."

The same evening, Santosh sat down to write another letter to his family – and this time he promised himself he would send it. He would tell them with pride about his achievements and his new friends and the good fortune that he had been blessed with. But what he really wanted them to know was that for the very first time in his life he felt he had risen above his condition as an untouchable. It almost seemed that in Thanjavur castes no longer existed. But this was an India so far removed from his parents' experience and so different to his father's view of life that he couldn't imagine how he could put it into words – at least words that his parents would believe.

CHAPTER 9
A LUCKY BREAK

On the Radapakkam road, one hot dusty day filled with the roar of the traffic followed another. But now, the second harvest of rice, for *Panguni*, was making full use of the local workforce. Most of the men and women from the surrounding villages were employed to gather the crop for the Rajah. The Rajah prided himself on being amongst the biggest rice producers of the state and thus played his part in making Tamil Nadu the number one rice producer in India. The workers surrounded the mechanical threshing machine – several dozen men and women in a symphony of colours – calling out to each other, and in good spirits despite their labours in the heat. As the jute bags used for storing the grain were filled, they were loaded onto the ox carts which stood in line, in the shade, the weary animals batting away the clouds of flies with a lazy swishing of their tails.

Ranji had still not figured out a way to sell his tyre and having temporarily abandoned his wood collecting for this better paid work, he was fully occupied in loading bags onto a cart when the Rajah Mokhtar's car rolled over the wooden bridge and then came to a stop in a cloud of dust in the loading area. The limousine, large and of a celestial blue colour, a Tata Indigo XL, was well known for being the most beautiful car in the area, its bodywork as dazzling as a mirror.

The driver opened the back door and assisted the Rajah in clambering out of the vehicle. Ranji set eyes for the very first time on this man – this most fortunate of all the notable men of the district. He wore dark glasses and had a large pot belly, which he had tried to conceal under a baggy white shirt. With his round face, his chubby cheeks and his long black moustache, Ranji noted he bore a strong resemblance to the portrait of Amresh Lal Nayar of the BJP, still there to be admired on posters which were left behind on the walls of Puttur, long after the election.

The Rajah had no need to call for Sharad Sarin, his foreman, as he was already hurrying forward, head bowed and with hands clasped in front of him, to welcome his superior. The workers also stopped their labour, and shielding their eyes with their hands, watched the scene. All of them had much the same in mind as evidenced by Sharad's enthusiasm: might there be some gain for them in this visit from the Rajah! The men tried to estimate the value of such a car and the number of lives they would need to live in order to afford it, and concluded that it was priceless.

Accompanying his words with expansive gestures, Sharad praised the progress of the work. A tall, thin man, with an angular face and a hooked nose, Sharad was feared by the workers for his unpleasant manner and his continual complaints. But now he was almost unrecognizable as he fawned, bowed and scraped to the owner. The Rajah asked questions, made comments. Sharad nodded his head enthusiastically in agreement. Ranji saw them approach the cart that he had just now finished loading up. His heart began to beat faster at seeing such a rich powerful man close up.

He stared intently at this little round man who hid his eyes behind dark glasses, spoke little and was now looking grimly at the portion of rice clasped in his hand.

God only knows why, but Ranji had imagined that wealth would surely paste a permanent smile on the faces of those who benefitted from it. He had believed that leisure would instil a perpetual good mood, and never having had the chance to test it out himself, he could not understand this scowl. For himself, if he had a quarter of an eighth of the fortune of the Rajah, he was sure he would spend his time smiling and joking with everyone!

What struck him most forcibly about the Rajah was his small stature. He was highly amused to see Sharad striving to bend at the knees so as to be at his boss's height, and Ranji, who was probably about as tall as the foreman, was delighted by this scene. There was at least one thing that he had more of than this richest of men! And the floral scent that he detected on him, quite unusual to his nose, seemed designed to attract interest almost as if to compensate for his unprepossessing appearance. He found it strange that a man like this had to resort to the kind of trick usually employed by women.

The Rajah, without a glance at him, had reached out a small hand towards a bag and had taken a handful of rice. He looked at it scowling and then, instead of putting it back in the bag, tossed it carelessly away from him as if to give it to the birds fluttering around them. Perhaps the grains were not big enough. Ranji stepped back, fearing that he was about to be subjected to some kind of reprimand.

Then his gaze, drawn irresistibly to the car so near, fixed on its tyres.

He was desperate to go closer to see them better. As the Rajah was now talking earnestly to Sharad and the conversation seemed to be all absorbing, Ranji cautiously approached the vehicle. He slowly crouched down in order to see better what was written on the side of the tyres. He recognised the letters that he knew now by heart: APOLLO.

Preoccupied by this deciphering he did not notice the Rajah turn suddenly, see him crouched against his car, and misinterpreting his interest, rush over with the obvious intention of connecting his foot with the backside of this shameless worker.

"What are you doing there, you scoundrel?" the great man cried, while Sharad also approached menacingly.

Shocked, Ranji rose but then, collecting himself, and as if not understanding the reproach, he smiled guilelessly at the owner:

"These are good tyres! Apollo tyres, enhanced with silicone, the high end!" he said, repeating what he had learnt from the *sadhu*.

"What? What are you talking about?"

Sharad roughly ordered Ranji to get away from the car and to get back to the field, but the Rajah silenced him with a gesture.

"What did you just say?" the great man addressed Ranji directly.

"The tyres on your car, Mokhtar *ji*, these are Apollo, made with silicone..."

"You...you know that? What's your name?"

"Ranji, Mokhtar *ji*"

"You know how to read but you are here loading bags onto carts?" pressed the Rajah.

"Yes, Mokhtar *ji*, I can read a little, but I can count very well! I have a friend who used to make tyres..."

The Rajah turned with a frown to Sharad Sarin repeating sarcastically as though he was truly puzzled: "He can read a little and can count very well! And you don't have a better job to give him than loading bags?"

Then, taking the arm of the foreman, they moved away from Ranji. The Rajah was asking what on earth this tyre expert was doing on his land. Sharad explained that he was only a seasonal worker and that the rest of the time he collected firewood to sell.

The landowner considered this. That the seasonal workers were illiterate didn't matter, but he knew that many of his permanent employees were also illiterate. He had here, an educated *dalit* who seemed to have passion and surely could be much better used in other tasks than to carry bags or collect firewood!

"This man deserves better than loading carts three times a year, Sarin! Does this mean you are unable to make the best use of the capabilities of my workers?"

"I didn't know about this man, Mokhtar *ji*..."

"I pay you to know! Take heed of my example and find this man a job matching his skills!" ordered the Rajah.

"Of course, Mokhtar *ji*. I'll take care of it. I'm sorry Mokhtar *ji*..."

A few metres away, Ranji was wondering bleakly if his boldness had cost him this job – would he be dismissed from the field? He was surprised to see Sharad come towards him, his face relaxed:

"You should have told me," he said. "Follow me!"

And he led him to the big shed where the crops were stored.

"This is where you are going to work now," announced Sharad Sarin with no further discussion.

CHAPTER 10
YOU'LL JUST HAVE TO
TRUST ME

Salaried employment might well have been a new gift from the gods, but it did not solve the problem of the tyre. And now here it was, taking up almost half the available space in the hut, as Meena never tired of pointing out. None of Ranji's initiatives so far had produced a result and, convinced that her husband would never find a buyer, she had started to insist that he should hide it outside, nearby if he so wished, just as long as she no longer had to breathe in the unpleasant smell of the rubber.

"Unpleasant smell?" thought Ranji. He couldn't agree with Meena's point of view. Compared with the stink of the sludge, the droppings of the animals, the fumes from the everlasting stream of passing vehicles – all of which they were used to, to the point of not noticing them anymore – the slight whiff of the tyre seemed to him like a fresh new and indeed pleasing smell ...of rupees.

At first Ranji insisted that it should stay in the hut; how could he leave something worth five thousand rupees in temptation's way? Eventually though, fed up with her continual nagging, he agreed that it should go outside. He lashed it securely to the trunk of the banyan tree with coconut ropes to ensure that no one could steal it. This gave Surya an idea. Why not make it into a swing just like the one she had seen in the yard of a house on her way to school?

Refusing outright to allow his potential cash windfall to be used as a plaything, Ranji continued with his search for a buyer. But after a month, Surya's insistence ground down even the obstinacy of her father. If using the tyre as a swing would amuse his daughter, why not grant her this pleasure while waiting for a buyer. So, taking care not to damage the plastic wrapping and the label, he consented to using a coconut rope to hang the monster from a large branch of the banyan tree. Recent events had certainly lessened his former urgency to convert it into hard cash, but the tyre still monopolized the family's attention despite having no customer. Occupying a place in the centre of family conversations, it was friction and arguments that it generated rather than rupees. Convinced that everything good that had happened to him stemmed from this huge round rubber object, Ranji vehemently insisted to his wife that, even if he had not yet realised the pile of money that it represented, it had already proved an effective talisman. The proof? The chain of events set off by its discovery had already resulted in him getting a job. A real job!

The fortuitous meeting with the holy man had exerted a very powerful positive influence on their destiny, he thought. Thanks to this tyre, he now received one thousand rupees every month as the head of the cashew pickers, and this without breaking his back or even wearying his legs. Because he could count and "read a bit," he had been given the job of recording the harvest per tree and per picker. And in addition, Sharad got approval from the Rajah for him to take home a bag of cashews if the expected yield was surpassed. It should be pointed out that this intervention by the foreman who, by the way, earned two bags for himself under the same conditions, was not entirely devoid of ulterior motives. In this way Sharad had someone else keeping a constant eye on the cashew gatherers, which meant he could go and drink his Kingfisher in peace at the bar of the nearby petrol station without his absence causing any decrease in the workers' yield.

But if the horizon had suddenly brightened for Ranji in one way, in another way he had good cause to feel anxious. He could never have imagined that his modest and recently acquired knowledge of tyres could produce such spectacular results. But now he was assumed to have skills that in reality he was far from possessing! Certainly he could count units and tens, certainly he could recognise some common words, but to weigh the bags, note the yields, and recognize the name of each picker, demanded a command of calculations and reading that he just didn't have.

Yet he accepted the job not only because the pink and white flowers appearing on the cashew crop announced an early harvest, but also because refusing such a proposal was impossible. "We do not discuss the orders of the Rajah!" Sharad had retorted when he had tried to explain that his knowledge fell well short of their expectations. Sharad was not an easy man to talk to and Ranji was unable to find the right words to express his position. It was quite impossible to tell the truth without risking his employment entirely.

Ranji had tried to explain that even if he knew something about cashew nuts, he knew absolutely nothing about cashew fruit. Sharad, who detected in him a malleable underling, swept aside the pretext:

"For the fruit it is exactly the same job, it's just that the cashew nuts are detached from them and put in a basket, while the fruit goes in a bag. As for you, you just count the bags and baskets that the workers bring you, and you weigh each one. Then, you note down the result next to the workers' names. It's simple but you must be very careful not to make a mistake."

Worried by the very likely possibility of confusion in this complex problem of accounting, Ranji prepared by putting in hours of study in his hut. He redoubled his interest in Surya's tuition, asking her to focus particularly on arithmetic operations as it was only in the addition of just two numbers that he was confident. In the evenings, stretched out under the bulb next to his daughter, he learned to do, and then redo, calculations with an "x" and horizontal lines, discovering multiplication and division which, according to Surya, would enable him to perform his work.

So by the time the harvest began a month before the monsoon was due, and thirty pickers were there shaking the cashew branches, Ranji was able to calculate the bags and the weights to the last comma. The first two days, he practised recognising the faces corresponding to the names written up on the board. When he was sure he had identified a picker, he added a cross next to his name. After a few days, his head full of names and the board full of numbers, he could give a good impression of really knowing how to read and to count.

The pickers' task was to gently detach the fruit so as not to damage them, to separate them from the cashew shells which they put into the baskets, then to bag up the fruit. Soon there were so many baskets and bags around Ranji that the thought of them made him dizzy.

Sharad came often to check up on his work during the first few days and appeared satisfied. After that, most days he went off on his motorcycle. From his breath when he

returned, Ranji realized where he had been: at the bar at
the service station. One of the labourers, Moopanar, confirmed that he had seen him there drinking with the truck
drivers. A vague idea started to take shape in Ranji's mind.
Undoubtedly Sharad was the boss. He had the power to fire
anyone who did not work as he should have, but he had
his own weakness: this was his predilection for leaving the
work in progress to go to drink at the petrol station. From
what Ranji had seen of his behaviour in front of the Rajah,
he was damn sure that Sharad himself could be fired if the
landowner had known of this practice.

Totally absorbed in keeping his accounts, he forgot
about the tyre during the day, but in the evening it was
always uppermost in his mind. By putting together Sharad
Sarin, petrol and tyres, the outline of an interesting plan
was emerging. If Sarin kept company with truck drivers,
maybe he could act as a go-between. It would be difficult
for him to refuse given what Ranji knew, and already Ranji
was speculating that this might be the chosen pathway for
the rolling of his Apollo Acelere. A hitherto unknown feeling of pleasure came over him as he considered that it was
just possible that the balance of power between him and his
boss might be tilting in his favour!

Spurred on by this discovery, he redoubled his efforts
to impress. His presence among the pickers, his continuous
coming and going amongst the trees encouraging the men
and women not to waste time, had a surprisingly positive
impact on their performance. However, in Ranji's mind, no
sense of ambition drove him to play at being the boss, he
was only motivated by his own desire to justify the trust that
had been placed in him. These bags that they were filling,
he compared to his own bundles of wood and he understood well the fatigue that sometimes overcame one of the

seasonal workers. So he encouraged them as he had been used to doing for himself until recently.

The resulting yields were so good that Ranji found himself rewarded with three big bags of cashew nuts that he carried jubilantly back to the hut.

Meena was soon surrounded by large quantities of cashew nuts but had very little idea what to do with them. At first she sold them in the same way as she used to when they had collected the fruits from the government owned trees. She sold them for just a few rupees, a few at a time, to pedestrians who passed by the hut, not concerned with how they were going to use them. Anyway every peasant of that area knew it would be unwise to consume them raw because until they are roasted they are toxic.

Then, one day, she saw some state workmen arrive in a van, and stop near the *kheti* with their ladders and baskets. They started to cut the tambour fruits from the trees surrendered to the state that had formerly contributed to feeding Ranji's family. Meena watched, sick to her stomach to see what they had lost. One of the supervisors, who seemed to be doing the same job as Ranji did for the Rajah, saw Meena's bags. Wondering how one so poor could possess such huge quantities of cashew nuts, he asked her where she had got her supplies. Meena explained. The man was wearing a madras shirt the colour of stone and a blue turban. He was smiling and seemed kind. Meena would remember him for a long time, because he bought a big bag of nuts from her for fifty rupees. How he must love them, Meena surmised and exclaimed.

"Oh no, I prefer peanuts! But I live in Tirulnelveti where my wife roasts them for spice merchants and tourists. They adore them!" replied the man unaware that he had given Meena a great money-making idea.

That same evening while Ranji was attempting a long division sum under the supervision of his daughter, Meena brought up the idea. Ranji frowned.

"I am sure that all it requires is two stones, a clay pot, a little wood and above all a good location. We have all that. I'm going to give it a go. What do you think?"

Ranji took off his turban and slowly scratched his shaven head, looking at his wife with a strange look. The image of a bus of pilgrims stopping with a swarm of women buying nuts to offer at the temple crossed his mind. Perhaps truck drivers would stop also, perhaps truck drivers in need of a spare tyre……

Meena was resplendent in a new sari. Accustomed to economising, she had opted for a plain green sari with just a simple gold border, but with a flirtatious smile on her dark face, she looked like a lady oblivious to the hardships of life. Her graceful neck, made muscular by her carrying, was slender and supple under her pretty face, framed by her hair, shining like onyx. Her stance showed off her breasts, pressed against her straw yellow *choli*, and her fine hands gracefully cupped her chin as her lively eyes sought an answer in those of Ranji.

"Who could resist such a pretty cashew saleswoman?" Ranji thought with pride, but even as this thought occurred to him, the vision dismayed him. Knowing that she would be exposed to the desires of passers-by prevented him from replying as he knew she wished. The advice of the rickshaw driver who used to live with them in Korrupet, the slum quarter of Chennai, came suddenly to his mind: "Don't marry a beautiful woman or you will regret it one day!" Ranji had certainly married a beautiful woman and he prayed he would never regret it!

"The wood, there isn't much left," he said.

"Enough to start with," countered Meena.

"And when there will be no more?"

"I will go myself to gather it," his wife rejoindered.

"You? And who will fetch water from the well? And the nuts, what will you put them in?"

"In plastic bags."

Ranji rubbed his chin.

"They say it can be dangerous when the shells explode," was his next attempt.

"No, not really. Not if you know what you are doing! It is the liquid contained in the shell which catches fire in the heat! I have seen it done many times by my aunt."

"Even so, it could be dangerous…"

At that Meena snapped: "Fine! You don't even want me to try it?"

That was exactly it! Feminine intuition almost always outwits the dull caution of men.

Subconsciously, Ranji felt that this activity might give his wife a freedom that he himself had lost in his new job. In exchange for earning regular money he had sacrificed his independence. Freedom came at a price! Since he had started working for the Rajah, he got up with the crows, splashed a little water on his face to wash, checked that he had his notebook in his shirt pocket, clipped on his ball-point pen, the symbol of his position, and went off, chewing a leaf of *tulsi*, to the orchards of the Rajah, to return only in the evening with his head stuffed full of figures. And even though the work brought regular money, it offered no discoveries, no surprises, nothing to lighten his heart.

When he collected wood, at least he could stop where he wanted and when he wanted, meditate or talk to anyone he wished. Nowadays, each day was exactly like the next.

He still hesitated about whether to agree to Meena's proposal. But the prospect of being able to afford the bicycle decided him.

"And how much would you sell a pound of roasted nuts for? Do you know?" he asked, just to test her true interest in this project one last time.

"And your bicycle? Do you know how much it costs?"

"One thousand two hundred rupees, with the panniers."

"So then? You tell me how much I should sell a pound for?"

"Okay!" He said, laughing. "I give up! You win!"

The very thought of having to divide the price of his bike by the number of pounds of nuts in the bags, made his head spin. But his pride quickly reasserted itself, and keen to gain the upper hand, he stated:

"Anyway, never mind about the bicycle, I'll buy it with money from the tyre!"

"My poor darling husband! Nobody wants your tyre! Believe me, if you want to ride your bike one day, you'll just have to trust me!"

Chapter 11
A Reversal of Fortunes

Meena had made a stove from an old clay pot no longer fit for cooking. Under the shade of the banyan tree, she had dug a fire pit in the red dust. A large flat stone protruding above it made for a hob and three smaller ones a tripod. It was rudimentary but functional.

Although Ranji had finally assented that she should try it to see how it went, this was mainly because it involved no financial outlay, just wood and the stones. It was also because he knew that his wife's family had roasted nuts so the technique was familiar to her – a knowledge that she had demonstrated when they could still harvest nuts from the state's trees. She used to grill them to complement her dishes, crushed and mixed with coconut oil. Added, along with chilli and fenugreek, these small comma-shaped seeds lent a nice crunchiness as well as flavour.

Her new venture had been slow to get started. Between fetching water, washing clothes in the river, doing the cooking and milking the cow there was never much time left for roasting nuts. Her method was to stoke the fire and stir the shells in the pot just until the point at which they caught fire and all became as black as coal. She needed to watch closely to make sure that only the shells were charred and that the nuts themselves did not burn. Then the earthenware pot was upended on the soil and a hundred smouldering coals were tipped out. Meena then cracked them open between two stones, taking care not to crush the precious seeds. It was a lengthy and messy operation and certainly filthy work but, attracted by the smell, people started to stop, to chat, and then to buy.

To begin with, Meena sold the roasted nuts wrapped in a large cashew leaf fashioned into a cone shape and fastened with a twig. Thirty rupees for a cone, which some saw as expensive though for others it seemed not too bad.

One day an elderly man stopped his tuk-tuk in front of the hut. Meena was crushing the shells. The customer took a cone and Meena, carrying on with her task, told him the price. Holding the cone in one hand, he looked for his money in his pocket and handed her three notes of ten rupees with a slightly shaky hand. But then, as he got back on his vehicle, the twig snapped and all the nuts fell on the ground.

Meena apologised and immediately handed him another cone. He thanked her and was about to leave when he turned back to her:

"My brother keeps a shop selling powders and other offerings at the Shiva temple in Puttur. If you're interested, I could bring you some transparent cellophane bags. They would be stronger than your cones!"

"I would love to have them," said Meena, "but surely they must be expensive!"

"All you would have to do is add on the cost of the bag. One or two *anna* more will certainly not discourage the hungry and anyway, you don't have any competition here! Next time I go, I'll bring you some. You can try them out."

Meena warmly thanked the old man, hoping that he would keep his word.

And he did! A few weeks later, he stopped again and gave Meena fifty small bags of different sizes. Meena, in exchange, gave him a cone filled to the very top. Without having any idea of the weight they might contain, she arranged her bags priced from three rupees for the smallest to fifteen rupees for the largest.

With the bags neatly arranged on a piece of board, her stall now looked very professional and the business grew. Ashok was one of those who stopped by very regularly.

Before, when passing by the hut, if he saw Meena busy with a household chore, he would call to her from the top of his wagon piled full of bricks. His compliments had made her uncomfortable.

"Hi there beautiful! So, will the evil Ravana ever succeed in capturing the beautiful sorceress? What do you think?"

Even though Meena did her best to ignore his allusions to the old story of Sita from the Ramayana she found it hard not to react and blush deep red. And Ashok continued on his way, delighting in her obvious embarrassment at his words. But the day that he had noticed, from far away, thick smoke enveloping the *kheti*, he struck the back of the zebu to get him there faster. Nearing the hut, he leapt from the cart and rushed over panic-stricken, believing that there was a fire and Meena might be in danger. And then he saw her in her fine sari, enveloped by smoke, stirring the clay pot. His relief was great as he realised his mistake.

Completely absorbed by this process, Meena did not at first notice that Ashok was there. He crouched down, transfixed, and his bright eyes stung by the smoke observed the charming spectacle.

Billows of smoke swirled around the *dalit* and she seemed arrayed as though for a performance of *bahrata natyam*, the classical fire dance in which the movements of the dancer evoke the flickering of a flame. Occasionally, the cloud was pierced by a glimpse of her beautiful face, intent on her work but shimmering in the rising heat like a drop of water in oil. At other times, lit up by the flare of a shell, it was her graceful body which emerged, moving like a dancer. Her arms described sparkling arabesques above the fire pit, no sooner appearing than being enveloped again by the thick smoke. Meena's movements were like an elegant puppet from a shadow theatre, a veiled goddess of incense ensconced within the heart of a *gopura* tower at the entrance of a temple.

Sometimes the swaying of her arms gave a hint of her breasts, round, perfect and generous as in statues of Parvati. Her curves stretched the fabric of the *choli* and what he could perceive made Ashok go weak at the knees.

"What are you doing here?" exclaimed Meena, suddenly realising he was there.

The *kshatriya's* look lingered on her, drinking in her body, up and then down. An unprecedented situation and impossible to satisfy his heart without transgressing the ancient rules.

"And you, pretty Meena? What are you doing?" Ashok croaked, barely above a whisper.

"You can see! I am roasting cashews," she answered, without looking at him.

"Did Ranji steal them?"

"Ranji is not a thief!" Meena replied, annoyed. "It is the fruit of his labour."

"Aha, so he works – that good-for-nothing!"

"Was it to buy nuts, or just to insult my husband that you stopped?" Meena asked sharply.

"Neither for one nor the other, princess!" retorted the bricklayer finding his spirit again.

He was watching her with the ambiguous smile that had so troubled Meena as they sat on the bench of his oxcart. And now the *kshatriya* was violating ancestral rules by looking straight at her, a lowly *dalit*!

The untouchable had the unpleasant impression that Ashok was undressing her in his mind! But there was something, divine or demonic, that attracted Meena to this man, and every time a shell exploded her heart gave a corresponding jump too. Maybe it was simply the pleasure of knowing herself to be desired, the pride in creating a strong feeling in someone of a higher caste. To be honest there was really nothing else about him that could justify this feeling. His untidy moustache, his cunning air, his insolent manner, none of these would have attracted Meena to Ashok, if it hadn't been for this barely concealed wolfish desire that he showed every time they met.

Now sitting idly on his heels as though he had nothing better to do, he seemed unaware of the ridiculousness of his situation, and certainly gave no thought to the former urgency of his delivery. Absorbed by lust, his thoughts travelled to forbidden shores, drawn irresistibly to this voluptuous woman sitting there stirring with her stick. How he would have loved to go further than looking and have fallen on these divine curves! He caught the scent of her embarrassment, and divining the torment hidden behind Meena's aggressiveness this added extra spice to his musings.

"So, where is he then with his cart?" he finally asked, with some idea of justifying his stop.

"His cart? What do you mean, his cart?" enquired Meena puzzled, raising her eyes towards him at last.

"Of course, yes. His cart. He was asking for information about the tyres of my one. He was looking into getting one, he told me."

"Oh, yes," Meena replied without fully understanding what Ashok was talking about. "I don't know... Now if you don't want to buy any nuts, perhaps you will be kind enough to leave me in peace to work!"

"I like watching you..."

"Well, that's as may be, but I am going to turn out the pot now and if you carry on standing there you may very well get burnt!"

A furious honking brought Ashok out of his state of blissful imaginings. He jumped up startled. And Meena burst into laughter at the sight of him sprinting towards his cargo that had moved away, and was plodding along right in the middle of the road, to the obvious annoyance of a bus driver.

"Get a big bag ready for me," shouted Ashok as he left.

That very first evening of roasting nuts Meena's fingers were sore. The smell of burning impregnated her sari and her hair, but she was thrilled to show Ranji the crumpled notes earnt from that day's labour. And every day they became more and more numerous. Ranji could hardly believe it: with the sale of her bags, Meena would soon be earning as much as him! His wife was doing well. She smiled more readily. Sometimes she hummed to herself. This successful start had transformed her, but even so Ranji sometimes asked himself if he hadn't preferred the situation before. Surya continued to do well at school: she had again brought home two candies for getting an A in reading and maths. But now there was a new factor in their lives: young companions, who had never before been seen at the *kheti*, were coming to laugh and play on

Ranji's tyre swing. This development upset his normal way of life.

Before this tyre transformed their existence, Ranji had lived with no other concern than that of feeding his family. Nowadays life seemed more stressful, more hectic, more complicated: his wife was now occupied with her new venture, and buses stopped regularly under the banyan tree. The children played boisterously with his tyre, and the cow, disturbed by all this activity, refused to eat. They felt the need to hide that they had more money because he knew that success bred gossip and envy. He constantly felt anxious, and had even resorted to cementing in place a mixture of mud and cow dung all around the perimeter of the hut to ward off the evil spirits that he had felt pressing in on them for some time. And as for him, he still hadn't got his bike, and so he was obliged to carry on going to the plantation to write down numbers in a notebook. There was nothing else for it.

The tyre hung as ever at the end of its rope and his hope of selling it one day dwindled even as the bags piled up in the warehouses of the Rajah.

But to make matters worse, three days ago Sharad had given him a dressing down for making a mistake. He had reversed two figures in the book, writing down 54 instead of 45 – and this was the second time it had happened. Suddenly the foreman was accused by the steward of not having checked the calculations. In turn, Sharad had accused Ranji of taking the goods. Ranji defended himself by citing the age of the scales, but he lost the bag of nuts which he should have got and, what was worse, he was immediately relegated to cutting the sugar cane.

He would like to have told Meena but he shrank from this admission of failure. Without a supply of nuts her business would cease and, if she had to pay money for them, it would be better that she did stop.

Demotion to the sugarcane crop was worse than the picking of cashew nuts. The workers had to cut through the sharp leaves, sharp as razor blades, all the while praying not to be bitten by the small green snakes that hid themselves in the hollow canes.

He had laid aside his notebook and pen and the next morning, bearing on his shoulders a shame that weighed more than any bundles of wood, he was to join the others in the cane fields for a harvest that would last until the monsoon.

How about turning down the job and returning to collecting wood? There was a thought. But even if he would earn less now, he had developed a liking for the comfort of the regular pay, and that he could even ask for an advance if he needed it. Suddenly the *sadhu's* warning popped back into his head. Could it be that he was right? Should one not even try to shape one's destiny but instead just accept and follow the course of one's life wherever it took you? But even as he thought this he dismissed it. The mistake he had made was surely no more significant an obstacle than a rock in a river. And water always finds a way to go around an obstacle. The route to his destiny would not be altered he was sure.

He was hoping that once his punishment was deemed to be over, Sharad would be forced to re-employ him, because, leaving aside these two mistakes, he knew he had made a big success of his role, and this was despite it being something completely new for him. He hoped that the Rajah would remember him and ask what had happened to him, and that he would judge the error to be tiny when set against the thousands of cashew bags stacked up in sheds all duly recorded. And that then the great man would tell Sharad to reinstate him to the accounting, as that was what they called the work. And so he reasoned it would be stupid of him to leave the Rajah's service just for a question of pride.

Tonight, he would tell Meena what had happened. He would tell her, once they were in bed, with Surya asleep on the rubber mattress that they had purchased from a hawker with money from the nuts. Tonight he would tell her, after slipping the roll of notes into the can of Pepsi, which served as a safe, hidden in its secret place. Tonight, he would tell her. But would he also tell her that perhaps, after all, money could not buy happiness?

CHAPTER 12
THE SEEDS OF DOUBT

One day soon after that, finding himself alone in the shed with Sharad, a rare occurrence, Ranji seized the opportunity to put a request to the foreman. Taking courage from his knowledge that he was an asset to his boss, he began with a discreet allusion to Sharad's frequent visits to the petrol station, and the fact that his absence left the workers unattended.

Sharad listened now with narrowed eyes, a slight smile on his lips. No need to say more, he understood well that the *dalit* was cunning and had something in mind. He would like to be the sub-foreman, that too. But Sharad knew something else too, which the *dalit* didn't know: the Rajah paid more attention to this man than he did to any of the other workers. Though he had certainly agreed that he should be punished for his miscalculations, he insisted that Sarin kept him occupied in this lower level task only as a temporary measure. Just a foible of the owner that Sarin attributed to Ranji's extraordinary performance with the tyres on his car.

"I have a small favour to ask," said Ranji, trying to make his voice sound less harsh.

"Yes, I got that! So? What is it?"

"When you go to the petrol station, you talk with the truck drivers, don't you?"

"Yes, sometimes," Sarin admitted. "Why?"

Ranji launched into his plan, and without revealing that he actually had one, he asked Sarin if he could make enquiries about a tyre if he gave him its characteristics.

"My word! Why on earth do you have this fascination with tyres?" exclaimed Sarin. "Do you also work for Tata or what?"

"I… I will tell you. But first could you find out if, by any chance, someone might need such a tyre?"

"Fine. I'll find out, but you'd better let me know why, huh? And every service has a price, right?"

Interesting how the opportunity to earn some money always changed things, thought Ranji. He had taken a gamble in stepping outside his usual submissive behaviour with his subtle but threatening hints. And it seemed to have excited some interest. New hope was born.

The next day, Sarin hailed Ranji from the path that led to the cane field and beckoned him over to join him. Machete in hand, the *dalit*, wiping his forehead, strode the hundred metres across the stumps of cut cane to approach the foreman.

"I have some news for you! You see, I am a man of my word!" Sarin said with that pretentious smirk which made him so dislikeable.

"So?" Ranji asked confidently.

"Those M385's are used on the old Russian trucks that the Army uses in north Kashmir."

"I didn't ask you about them!" Ranji responded, already irritated.

"Aha! Not that much of an expert in tyres now, my friend!" crowed the foreman. "Your Apollo and the M385, they are the same thing! Surely you must know that Mr Specialist!"

Ranji was ill-equipped to deal with this mockery. Of course he had heard of Kashmir, even though it was the state furthest away from Tamil Nadu, and he knew that it had been plagued for half a century by the struggle between India and Pakistan. There would certainly be lots of army trucks there but it was unthinkable even to imagine that he could sell his tyre there! A fatal stab to his hopes. Crushed, the machete now hung loose from his hand, and his face was a picture of misery as he took in this news. But Sarin continued,

"Come on! This is just the start of it! Here's some other information for you. Some of these vehicles have been sold to companies working with stone or cement because they are nigh on indestructible."

"Really?" Ranji felt a faint glimmer of hope.

"And it seems that some are used in the Ghats to transport the pink granite boulders and in Wayanad to carry logs of teak and cullenia," Sarin finished triumphantly.

Sarin was not the boss for no reason. Though his education had probably not extended further than college, he knew about things completely unknown to Ranji. The *dalit* could sense Sarins's advantage here by the tone of voice employed, like that of a teacher as he showed off his superior knowledge, and at the same time, the reminder he gave that they belonged to different social castes.

This mountain chain of the Western Ghats was a mystery to Ranji. He knew that the mountains called Nilgiri were located to the north of the state, and that the pink stone of the temple of Gangaikondacholapuram came from there, but he was not really sure exactly where the Nilgiri were, and even less so the Wayanad district.

"Oh, that's very far away," he said, very aware of his ignorance. "It's not useful information for me."

"That's as may be! You asked me for a piece of information, I give you three facts and you want to scoff at it? Now, are you going to tell me why you're so interested in those pesky tyres?"

So far Ranji had not shared his secret with anyone except Meena. But over time, he had come to the inescapable realisation that without help from someone better placed than him, he was never going to be able to sell the tyre. And he had at least managed to pique the interest of Sarin.

"I have one," he said wearily, "and I want to sell it."

"Aha! So that's it! And where do you keep it?"

"That's my business. But if you can find me a buyer, I will give you some of the money," replied Ranji, finding again a little spirit.

"How much?" Sarin demanded.

"Find a customer first," replied Ranji encouraged by Sarin's sudden interest.

Sharad frowned and looked displeased. He felt he should have the advantage here and had no intention of being manipulated by this cane cutter.

"I did exactly what you asked me to do, and what do I get? Nothing, except a request for another favour! If that's how you expect to do business, you'd better talk to someone else!" And as he sensed a coup, Sarin added,

"If I find you a client, it's half for me."

"A quarter," Ranji shot back without thinking.

"A third. That's my last offer. And now get back to work, otherwise I will have to dock you an hour's pay."

"Have you got an idea of how to sell it?"

"That's my business now," retorted Sharad maliciously, "you'll just have to wait and see. OK?"

Hope having regained the upper hand, Ranji accepted this and returned to the field. He repeated the mechanical gesture, slicing and binding the purple stems with the dexterity of an experienced wood cutter. But, his mind was far away, and his lack of attention to the task meant he cut his left hand many times because the leaves were sharp as razors. He could think of nothing but the conversation he had just had. And one particular word had reawakened something in his memory: cement. And as he had made Surya read Santosh's letter close to a hundred times, he knew that his son had mentioned cement deliveries.

He wanted to act on this thought immediately and almost wished he had not already put Sarin on the case, because now the seed of an idea was suggesting a possible solution closer to home. For it had occurred to him that Santosh himself might well have access to the contacts which he had been so desperately seeking for months. And even if his son's distance made this impossible, another cement connection might be available through Ashok who he knew went regularly to deliver bricks to construction sites, and construction sites also used a lot of cement!

Ashok! Him again! Unthinkable to ask for another favour from that arrogant man. Ranji already owed him a debt of honour which he had no idea how he would repay. Also, for a reason which he couldn't altogether put his finger on, he was wary of the brick maker, and his womanising reputation made him even more unsympathetic. Must he once again ask for help from this cocksure man, and abase himself before him? And what would Ashok ask for in return? Certainly as much as Sarin, maybe even more …

The night before, when Surya was finally asleep, he and Meena had turned out the can and they had counted, for at least the tenth time, their savings. Eight hundred... mostly in crumpled notes of ten rupees. Even including those earned by his wife, which he would prefer not to touch, he was still at least four hundred short of the price of a bike. The stock of nuts was running out but as long as the great monsoon didn't arrive before October, then there was still a very small chance they could raise the necessary amount just before the rains started.

If he sold the tyre for two thousand five hundred rupees, he would have to give eight hundred and forty to Sarin, still leaving him with one thousand six hundred and sixty! More than enough to buy the bicycle, buy the presents he had planned and, perhaps, buy a second younger cow.

And between Ashok and Sarin, which one offered the best chance of success? The least unpleasant option was undoubtedly Sarin, and perhaps, Ranji tried to convince himself, he was in the best position, in that, as an owner of a motorbike, he could go wherever he wanted. He did well to strike a bargain with him. But he would still ask Surya to write that letter to Santosh.

A future for the tyre seemed to be emerging. The approach of the monsoon was coming too. The monsoon that could destroy a whole crop, annihilate a herd or devastate a village, with its torrential rains and violent winds. He dreaded it. Some of the money would have to be used to cover the hut with plastic sheeting, and more must go to consolidate its structure, because when the wind blew, it was not uncommon to see the roofs of huts scattered in the sky like giant crows. He had already put aside a few of the blue plastic bags that were used to protect the bunches of bananas and which would offer good protection from the rain, but as they would fly away easily, they would have to be secured well. He decided he must speak to his old friend Vicash who had relatives working in the banana plantation.

"I have never eaten such magnificently roasted cashews!" exclaimed the brick maker. "I would like three of your big bags! I guess I will get a special price for that?"

"I can only give you two, Ashok."

"What! For such a good customer as me?"

"I am running out of stock, sorry."

Meena told a small lie. She still had one large sack, but she did not want him to believe that he was entitled to preferential treatment. For weeks he had stopped to buy a bag of roasted nuts almost every day. And every time she met his eyes, on taking the money, he brought turmoil with him too. And ripples spread through her body, tensing up her stomach, making her neck stiffen, causing her hands to tremble.

Ashok made her feel uneasy but he was undoubtedly a valuable customer. A shudder seized her when she saw the red and blue tipped horns of his zebus approaching on the road from behind the banyan tree. In her anticipation of these meetings – because she did look forward to them despite feeling anxious – she found it impossible to discern if this stemmed from a legitimate business reason or from another feeling, much more complicated, which sowed confusion in her mind. Sometimes she enjoyed being alone with this man who showed her many kindnesses quite apart from the rupees, something which Ranji now seemed incapable of doing. She knew she was desired and found beautiful by someone new, while her husband seemed to have abandoned her in favour of a large round lump of unsaleable rubber.

In the past, her husband's imagination had taken them to the heights, extreme moments of pleasure that transcended their material conditions. But since he had started working for the Rajah, the formerly ardent Ranji had lost his appetite. To be honest, his mind now seemed absorbed by too many new things: calculations for example. Since he had learnt how to manipulate numbers in this way he spent all his time applying these rules and calculating everything. Then the upheaval in his daily life, caused by his new status of employment by the Rajah, and this recent mistake, for which he was being punished, continued to torment him. He seemed desperate to take up his notebook and ball point pen again, and he talked incessantly of nothing else......Apart from the damn tyre which he imagined already sold!

And it was towards this tyre that Ashok looked then, seeming to notice it for the first time.

"Say, that's a funny swing that thing there! Looks like a tyre..."

"Well, that's because it is!"

"And what's more, it doesn't look worn. But..." Suddenly Ashok associated the object with Ranji's approach to him and his famous 'investigations'.

"Aha! I get it now," he said with a self-satisfied nod.

"Ranji intends to sell it, but until then Surya and her friends can enjoy it."

"And I wonder how your stupid husband will ever manage to make that happen!"

"Ashok! I have already asked you not to insult Ranji! And now go away and leave me alone, please!"

But instead of getting up to go, Ashok stayed sitting in front of Meena and stared at her with his charming but exasperating smile:

"I have recent news of Santosh," he said, confident that he would capture her interest now.

Meena's eyes widened with pleasure. In that instant her anger faded. She crouched down next to him, and her eyes sought out those of the brick maker.

"Couldn't you have started with that?" she asked, in a tone of gentle reproach.

"It seems that he works in an office now."

"In an office? What do you mean….in an office?"

"Someone told me that when I was delivering at the building site of the Royal Orchid hotel. Things are going well for him. But for you too, it seems. The cashew business seems to suit you! You are more beautiful than ever…"

Embarrassed, Meena immediately averted her gaze. No, he was not a handsome man, with his pock-marked cheeks, badly concealed under his three-day old beard. And he was incredibly forward. When women spoke about him at the well, there was always one telling how he had been beaten up for having seduced a married woman. It looked like the need to seduce ran in his veins like blood. Maybe it was an incurable disease.

"And what does my son do in this office?"

"Ah! That I don't know! Maybe he only serves the tea, or sweeps the floor. But what about your cane cutter? It seems that he lost his nice job!"

Right then Indra arrived, always at the place where you didn't want her, at exactly the moment when you didn't want her. Always quick to work out what was going on behind the conversation, always mischievous and keen to spread gossip. Inexhaustible on the exploits of men who climbed coconut trees during the day and rested at night. Her stories made the younger women blush and the older ones who could guess at the fibs, laugh.

Indra was not only a good storyteller, she had a finely developed sense of observation. Women sought her company because she made them laugh but, at the same time they were wary of her. Laughter served as the riches of the poor: snatching at those moments of collective joy, sorrows disappeared. Recently Meena had felt herself to be targeted by Indra's insinuations. She knew that with little effort, Indra could whisk up a romantic epic to delight the whole village. She sniffed it out, Indra, and she sniffed like a dog at the little story Ashok was writing with Meena.

"So cousin," she said to Ashok, "you love cashew nuts now?"

"And it looks like you do too," Ashok retorted.

"I came by to say hello to my girlfriend," said his cousin.

"Well I am just buying her nuts, and I am sure that my visit to Meena is more useful than yours."

"Maybe, but you may judge mine even more useful to you!" said Indra with a laugh.

"Really! I doubt it!" snapped back Ashok.

"You must really adore those nuts to drop a cartload of bricks on the road!" said Indra, motioning with her head towards the road.

Ashok turned round to look, concerned. No, this could not be possible! He had taken care to tie up the animals this time, though maybe he had done so a little hurriedly. But the cart was definitely missing.

He rushed over to the road. The load was definitely moving in the wrong direction.

"It's not like him to be distracted like that!" Indra remarked sarcastically. "And it seems that it is not the first time!"

"He came to give me news of Santosh," said Meena, feeling her cheeks turn red.

"So, it seems that bringing you news of your son was so important that it made him forget his own business. Unless it is your business that interests him more than anything..."

"Indra!" Meena exclaimed.

"Come on, I'm kidding, I hope everything is going well for your son. A handsome boy – he gets his looks from his mother!"

And Indra passed on by, laughing at her own witticisms, while a jam formed behind the cart which Ashok was struggling to bring back under control.

CHAPTER 13
STEP BY STEP

Sitting on the tow bar of the cart, Vicash and Ranji were going to the sugar mill, with a cargo of sugar cane so huge that the lower stalks swept the road while the highest disturbed the birds in their branches. Two scrawny little zebu towed the swaying load.

Vicash was pretty much the only person that Ranji really trusted. When he and Meena had settled in the area, several years earlier, Vicash had been one of the few to show him some kindness. Vicash was a herdsman so he knew about cattle, but he was changing his occupation from tending the cattle to using a cart and his oxen for transport. Vicash loaned Ranji some money and sold him a cow. A few years older than Ranji, he was the kind of friend who went a long way to compensate for the lack of relatives. Ranji had repaid him over the years with milk and with the money he made from selling the fruit. Ranji valued their friendship highly and recognised its worth, but he had not yet spoken to him about the tyre.

"The other day I went to buy some chickpeas in Puttur," said Vicash, "and I was drinking tea at Good Karma, the cafe next door. There were two men who were arguing. The older one was wearing a badly fastened turban and *vesti* as dusty as ours. His eyes were burning red and his mouth was bleeding. The other one was wearing smart trousers and a shirt ironed as if it had come straight from the laundry. The gold buckle on his belt sparkled and shone brilliantly like the Rajah's car. He was carrying a small leather brief-case which he waved around while he was speaking. I soon realised that he was the son of the old man. He was trying to convince his father that he should have his tooth extracted because it was causing him so much pain."

"And? What happened?" enquired Ranji.

"The old man didn't want to do it. He said the pain was part of his karma. 'We are born, we die, we are reborn, and the more I suffer in this life then the better my new life will be.' That was what I heard him stammer even as he was spitting out blood. Do you believe that is true?"

"Yes. Don't you?"

"It's not what my cousin Tarun thinks. He says we should rebel against the idea of reincarnation," answered Vicash.

"Tarun? Is that the one in the Communist Party?"

"Yes, that's right. He works for the state, in the road department. But he is a good Hindu anyway. He even joined the last *Kumbh Mela* pilgrimage."

"So he still has some belief then. But anyway, how can any of us know for sure?"

While Ranji thought about this, he stroked his chin with his thumb as if this movement might help to clear the fog from his thoughts. This rubbing of his stubble produced the same noise as that of a sickle mowing wheat. This familiar sound accompanied his musing: should one really believe in the role of suffering in gaining for oneself a better life once reincarnated? He had been struck by recognising on the Rajah's face something that looked very much like suffer-ing, and he was pondering that perhaps it was related to the human condition regardless of caste, wealth or karma. But how could that be fair? Surely in terms of suffering, what with the pneumonia of a child, the constant irritation of a gastric upset, and on top of that the daily battle to feed his family, he had had his fill. If returning to earth meant to start again a life like this, perhaps it would be better to stay dead forever.

"Well, whatever the truth is, that son – he was lucky to have a father. I would have liked to get advice from one, and to be able to give it to him later on," Ranji said.

"You didn't have a father?" asked Vicash.

"No, just a mother. From what she told me, she was attacked by an unknown man in an infamous alley in Teynampet, and I was the result. As for her, my mother, I acted as the bait for her begging near the temple in Mylapore. We slept in the street not far from the Adyar, and I have happy memories of that river because we, the children of the poor, loved to swim in it. One day, when I must have been about five years old, I got a fever and started to cough. My mother used all her savings to take me to the clinic. The driver of the tuk-tuk, Deepak, took pity on this girl and her brat and he took us under his wing. We went to live with him in a tin shack alongside the railway tracks. For him it was convenient, he jumped aboard the carriage as it was passing by and went to work without paying an *anna*. But it didn't last. After that my mother and I, and my little brother, we went to the west…"

"So was that where you started to work?"

Ranji concurred. "Yes, I guess it was – but as a collector! I've always liked to find a use for things that others throw away. I didn't like the selling part so much but I did manage to earn a few *naye paise* from the things that people threw out of the train windows. It was later on, when I was fifteen or sixteen, that I worked for the first time on the harvest."

"The gods must have been watching over you. You have a wonderful family now."

"I have to believe that if you behave as well as you can in this life, you will have a better life when you come back," said Ranji. "Maybe it's not true. Maybe your cousin Tarun is right, but as for me, I perform *puja*, I pray to the gods and now I have to wonder at what has happened to me: first, a tyre fell off a truck! Then I met a wise man, and thanks to the wise man, I impressed the Rajah, and thanks to the Rajah, I got a job on his payroll. So, is there any point in suffering as your old man does with his teeth, when a dentist can extract them easily? I don't know. For him, his sorrow is the pain he feels because of his rotten teeth, for me at the moment it is the lack of a bicycle. And if I have one, one day, it will be because the gods want me to have it. Does it change anything in my reincarnation?"

"You speak good sense when you want to," Vicash remarked, but he made no reaction to Ranji's reference to the tyre.

"I speak easily with you, because you are my friend."

"That is true. I too believe that there is no life without suffering. It is faith that helps us to bear it," concluded Vicash.

Ranji had nothing to add. His friend had lost his two eldest sons. The first was hit by a reckless driver, the second drowned in the great flood of the Cauvery. And hardly better off than him, he now had only one son, and a little girl Gitika, Surya's best friend. Despite these terrible things that had happened to him, Ranji had never heard Vicash complain about anything. He was the kind of man who showed a natural empathy for people and kept his problems to himself. So Ranji greatly appreciated that he was now sharing his thoughts about reincarnation. Maybe he was secretly concerned as to what his sons' new lives on earth were like. Or indeed if they even had one.

It was Vicash who broke the silence as they approached Ranji's hut:

"At the end of the day, whatever the suffering, however severe the pain may be, the thing that is most remarkable is that in the end you get so used to it that you almost forget about it."

Ranji gave a nod of his head. He agreed with his friend.

Whilst overtaking them, a huge bus unleashed an impressive diesel fart and they were enveloped in the thick oily smoke. A passenger yelled something inaudible from behind his window. Another bus approached, decked with orange banners, as though bound for a pilgrimage, whilst a colourful truck, stuck behind a cohort of motorcycles, desperately honked its horn like a ship in the mist, to claim its right of way. Pedestrians passed by, stopped, chatted and went on again like ants exchanging pheromones.

"How is your son getting on?" asked Vicash.

"He has a good job now," responded Ranji proudly.

"How long has he been away?"

"Seven months exactly, the 6th day of Ashwin Vad."

"That long!" exclaimed Vicash.

"The day after his departure, it was raining. It felt as if he had disappeared under the waves," replied Ranji sadly.

Seven months! An eternity. Ranji recalled his son's youthful smile as he climbed up onto the truck, in his new clothes bought in the end for one hundred and twenty rupees from the tailor's shop in Puttur. A considerable amount and one that seriously depleted the savings for the bicycle. And he recalled how happy his son had looked, as if he had captured the heart of a princess, and the water all around aflutter with migratory birds. Thinking about it, a feeling of great sadness gripped his stomach. He had always hidden his own anxiety in order not to increase that of Meena, and always gave the impression that he was glad about his son's departure in search of new opportunities. But yes, it had been a difficult moment, and the silence that followed had given rise to uncertainty, nibbling away at that false good mood, until the arrival of that wonderful liberating letter. And then at last he knew it had been the right choice. But it still didn't take away the melancholy of his boy's daily absence.

"Of course if you had him here, he would be able to help you," said Vicash.

Arriving level with his *kheti*, Ranji jumped down from the cart to remove two or three canes from the load to leave at the foot of the banyan. It was what he normally did, a few missing canes would not ruin the owner.

Meena was not there. The stall had been packed away. Under the blackened pitcher he saw that the fire had gone out. The fabric was drawn closed at the entrance to the hut. Ranji moved it aside. No-one inside. She must have gone to market, he thought. And as he thought it he realized that for some time, they had led their lives almost independently of each other. Sometimes the strange feeling that they had nothing to say to each other came to him at night, when they found themselves lying side by side on the mat, tired from their days, as if their only common interest was concentrated in a can of Pepsi buried in the earth. Even Surya was different from the way she was before. The swing didn't entertain her as much as at the beginning – that big ridiculous tyre hanging uselessly at the end of the coconut rope instead of turning on a Russian truck…

"So that's what you are trying to sell," commented Vicash, motioning towards the tyre with his chin.

"You know about it?"

"Ranji! Do you think our girls are so silly that they don't know what is going on? Of course I know about it, but you didn't tell me yourself, so I respected your silence."

"You are right. And a friendship like ours goes a long way towards making up for suffering. It fell off a truck one evening of *Ekadashi*. Nobody came back to look for it. Ever since then, I've been obsessed with working out how I can sell it. Thank you for keeping quiet but now, as you know about it, how about you tell me what you would do in my place?"

Vicash slackened off on the reins, and the axles whistled again like poorly lubricated gears as the zebu moved forward. After a while the sugar mill appeared ahead of them at the bend in the road. Huge billows of white steam were emitted by a tall chimney, while the sweet smell of burnt sugar hung heavy in the air.

"It's a shame that it is so big!" said Vicash finally, referring to the tyre.

"Don't tell me about it!"

"Why not see if the manager at the petrol station is interested?"

"I have asked Sharad Sarin to find out."

"Why don't you go yourself? We could put it on the cart," suggested Vicash.

Ranji turned towards his friend, showing a sad and hollow face, stubble from a week's growth, and indicated his shirt in tatters and his filthy turban.

"An outcast like me, you can imagine their faces when I tell them: 'Hi, I'm Ranji and I have an Apollo Acelere M385 / R80 tyre for sale.' They will immediately jump to the conclusion that I stole it! At best, they'll laugh at me, at worst they'll call the police. I think it's better to let Sarin do it."

"I guess that makes sense. So what are you planning to do in the meantime?"

"I will carry on cutting the canes, taking them to the sugar mill with you, and I shall wait, but I am thinking."

"Thinking about what?" asked Vicash.

"To be honest, Vicash, I'm not sure I have actually resigned myself to doing this job. When I was picking up dead wood, it's true I didn't earn much, but at least there was no one to tell me what I should be doing. I would have seen a dead branch, like that one there, I would have waited for it to fall in the first gust of a strong wind, and then with my machete I would have cut it into two nice logs. And if I needed help in taking it to the hut we would have come across each other on the way, you would have helped me and we would have smoked a *beedi* together and had a chat."

"Don't think about things too much, Ranji. The less you think, the less complicated things will be. Look at the faces of people who work in the city. It is clear that they think all the time! This is where all the problems come from! You and me, we are just poor people, but our lives are simple: we feed our families and we don't have all their worries!"

"It's good advice. I'd love to think less, but it seems to be more powerful than me and getting worse since I found this tyre."

"Be like my zebu! They don't think. They just go forward step by step! But in fact, I'm going to stop them here. Could you get down and lead them from here to the mill? The turning to the entrance is difficult and I don't want to drop my pile of cane."

Ranji took charge of the animals by walking at the side of the cart with its rickety load and successfully negotiated the turn to get into the sugar mill. Other carts were parked in disarray, waiting for their turn to get their cargo weighed. Vicash halted the animals.

"You know," said Ranji, "About Santosh – he can still help me, even though he is not here. Wherever it is he works, he knows about cement…"

They finished delivering their last load a little before nightfall. On the way back Vicash dropped Ranji off at his hut. One of the good things about his new job was that he got home early enough to see Surya and talk to her about her day. It strengthened their relationship for him to know about the things his daughter enjoyed and to hear what she had learnt at school. He always paid close attention and in that way he too had learnt much about the history of their country, had discovered the complex social structures, and even learnt something more about the geography. Sometimes she taught him the meaning of a new word, but today it was he who had something to pass on, and Surya could be very useful to him.

While he and Vicash had been unloading their second delivery, a large truck covered with religious slogans had come to park in the dusty courtyard of the sugar mill. As he did whenever possible, Ranji went surreptitiously to inspect the tyres of the truck, and – what a surprise! – he recognized the magical signs imprinted on his memory: APOLLO Acelere M385 / R80 / 22.5! He looked tenderly at this truck that gave credence to his project. So there definitely were vehicles driving with *his* tyre in the vicinity! Unfortunately, the driver wasn't there and he could not question him because he did not return before they left. Nevertheless, finding that reinforced his hope of getting some help from Santosh.

As he dismounted from the cart he saw Meena, holding the bucket with the milk from that evening in her hand.

"Hi Meena! Have you had a good day? Where is my adorable little girl?" called Ranji cheerfully, arriving at his cabin.

"Surya's not here. She went with Arun and Uma to watch Traffic Signal, a film showing on Star One. I agreed to it because it is a story about poor people, like us, who live in a big city…"

Sometimes, when there was an amusing or educational film, Uma's parents, who had a small business selling spices and dried fruits in the village, invited Surya to their home. They paid seventy-five rupees per month to receive forty television channels and one of the two rooms of their house was often used as a movie theatre for family and friends.

Ranji's mood turned black, and Meena sensed this but could not understand this sudden change.

"Have I done something wrong?" asked Meena.

"No … not really; well yes, because I need her."

On the fire, shallots were sizzling in coconut oil. Meena was a master of multi-tasking. She poured the milk into an earthenware pot which she had already wet thoroughly and placed in a draught to keep it cool, and then added two handfuls of black lentils, a pinch of turmeric, a piece of tamarind and some ginger to the softening onions before asking Ranji:

"What do you need her for?"

"I think I have found the answer!" said Ranji.

"The answer? To what?"

"To what! To the sale of the tyre, of course!"

"Your tyre! Always your damn tyre! What is it you think you have found out now that you have such an urgent need for Surya?" snapped Meena.

"I want her to write a letter to Santosh."

Meena whirled round to face him and spoke sternly:

"Oh no! You're not going to bore Santosh with this story as well now! He has a serious job to do, and he must concentrate on it. Leave him alone and muddle through this on your own!"

Ranji, surprised by this new found aggressiveness, stared at his wife, bewildered. He suddenly noticed the *tilak* on her forehead: a red dot, and the three horizontal lines of ash: the *tripundra.*

"You went to the temple of Shiva?"

"And how does that concern you? Yes, I went to give thanks for our great good fortune and to meditate," Meena replied dryly.

"Meena!" exclaimed Ranji, astonished by her tone.

"What now?"

Ranji was not used to seeing his wife in this state. He saw contempt on her face. He caught the penetrating light that flashed out from Meena's dark eyes, like that seen in a *Brahmin's* eyes when you get in his way. Faced with this verbal abuse, Ranji could take in the words, but he didn't understand what could have brought about this sudden revolt, especially after going to the temple. An appalling thought came to him: could she possibly have become involved with someone else?

"I came by the hut this afternoon…"

Now Ranji raised his voice too. After all, who was the head of the household? Did she think that she could now speak to him in that way just because she made a contribution to the household income? Did she believe she could address him like that and do whatever she wanted just because she brought in a few rupees with her nuts?

"And?"

"You weren't here…"

"No. I was in the temple with the pilgrims."

"So, the cashews, it's over? You're going into town while I work! Spending our money no doubt!"

Meena, now furious, got to her feet.

"Did you really forget that it was the day of the pilgrimage to Sri Rangam? It's been months since we talked about anything to do with the village! Two buses arranged to take everyone, and you, you see nothing, you hear nothing, you're lost in dreams of your rubber pudding! And to top it all now you accuse me of spending the little money that I earn from my work!"

"Listen Meena, I'm tired. My arm hurts from using the machete. I loaded and then unloaded three carts full of cane with Vicash, so, please, I beg you, give me a break! Okay, I should have remembered this pilgrimage, but now I have to send an urgent letter to Santosh, because I know how I can sell the tyre!"

"Well, it will have to wait till tomorrow."

"I need to find a quick solution, Meena. And to write the letter will not take her very long," insisted Ranji.

"Spending our money!" fumed Meena. "You complain to me that you are tired, but what about me? What should I say? I roast the nuts, I milk the cow, I wash your clothes. I do the cooking! I carry the water and sweep the hut! But do you hear me complaining?"

"I am not complaining. I was only saying that I need Surya back here to write an urgent letter to Santosh. Looks like, despite this *tilak* on your forehead, the expedition has put you in a very bad mood! Has something happened?"

Meena stifled her anxiety. Of course something had happened, but she would not tell him anything. Her anger masked an inner turmoil.

"It's because of you and your damn tyre. The earth has stopped turning since you met the *sadhu*. Nothing else interests you, and as for me, I do not even exist! You are possessed by a *shaitan*, my friend. It was to lift that curse that I went to do *puja*!"

"Nonsense!"

"You didn't even notice the bricks."

"Bricks! What bricks?"

"The bricks out there that ... that Ashok gave you."

"Ashok gave me bricks?" exclaimed Ranji. "Has he gone mad, or what!"

The knot in her stomach clenched tighter. Meena had her back to the wall. She knew very well why Ashok had come to leave her those bricks.

"He said you had given him wood for a favour that was not worth it. It is in preparation for the monsoon, to protect the hut from flooding..."

"Why did you agree? I don't want to be in debt to that man. That's why I gave up a day's work for him! To protect us from flooding indeed! What is this really about?"

Even as his anger rose, a terrible suspicion dawned and Ranji's eyes widened in horror. No, surely even that lout would not dare to try to buy the favours of his wife! But what was Meena hiding from him? He knew her well enough to know there was something.

"I'm going to take them back," he said firmly.

Meena had known he would react like this. She had tried to dissuade Ashok who had come and smilingly deposited fifty bricks at the side of the hut without even asking her opinion, but she could not stop him. Behind her anger she was hiding her own bitterness at having failed to refuse this poisoned chalice.

"Meena!"

"Yes."

"No. Nothing ... Anyway, what time will Surya get back?"

"She's going to sleep there. Uma's father will take them to school on his motorcycle."

"OK, fine! So what I might want, it counts for nothing? It would be better for her to do her homework and go to bed early. I might need her! Anyway, I do need her, to write this letter."

"Look at this!"

Meena had rushed into the hut and emerged brandishing a piece of paper with narrow blue lines.

"What is it?" said Ranji, but with little curiosity.

"Her report card. See this: 'A'; here, here and here!"

Ranji, lost for words, recognized the same notation on all lines.

"She read aloud to me what is written underneath by the lady: 'Surya is the best student in her class.' This is why I allowed her to go with Uma and to stay to sleep there."

Ranji's eyes misted up as he examined this piece of paper. His anger had disappeared as fast as does a sparrow. He was so proud of his little girl! All his sacrifices had not been in vain.

"You did well!" he conceded, "And you are right…"

"So, are you hungry? The lentils are cooked," was Meena's final grudging question.

Inside the hut, the only sound came from the traffic outside. With nightfall its flow seemed to have reduced a little. They paid it little attention, except when their own silence became deafening. Ranji dipped his hand into the softened lentils to form a ball with his fingers and brought it slowly to his mouth. Meena's slim glass bracelets tinkled against each other as she did the same. The absence of Surya, which should have brought them closer together, seemed instead to push them apart. Both of them seemed to be chewing on something other than food. Each brooded to themselves on the things that irritated them in the other, but they said nothing. Then their thoughts moved seamlessly on to the things they did like, and the balance gradually tilted the other way. Ranji was grumpy, but so kind! Meena was hot-tempered, but what a worker! Ranji wondered if he should abandon his tyre, get rid of it forever. Meena asked herself if she should ever have started with this venture of roasting nuts.

They were lying on the *charpoi* of string, without exchanging a word, angry as much with themselves as with each other, dwelling on this insidious rancour which they were incapable of overcoming with words. They both pretended to fall asleep with their backs to each other, but the noise of their breathing revealed that they were still awake, and their state of mind denied them the comfort of sleep. Then, late at night when the noise of the trucks was spaced by intervals of silence, they finally fell asleep.

Ranji was awakened some time later by the gentle snoring of his wife. He felt her warm presence against his body. His hand touched Meena's arm, gently stroked the texture of her skin, smooth and soft. The weak moonlight that entered through the opening in the hut lit up her pretty sleeping face. His princess slept quietly in his arms. He regretted that stupid argument. Of course Meena was right. Whether the letter was written tonight or tomorrow, what did it matter? A sweet feeling of harmony pervaded the hut, unlocked by their embrace. The divisive issue of the tyre had vanished into the night leaving in its place a gentle soothing feeling.

Driven by a spontaneous desire for tenderness, Ranji curled up against the body of his wife and pulled her closer to him. Meena woke without opening her eyes and snuggled against Ranji. The moistness of their skin mingled to form one common film of sweat as they clung intimately to each other, just as the sap seals the sapwood tree. They were united, stronger than ever because able to overcome their conflicts. At the end of the day, wasn't that the point?

He hugged Meena more tightly and she opened one eye. His eyes shone in the darkness, black pearl set in its nacre shell. She took his hand, rough and coarse from his numerous cuts, and moved it gently over her body as if to comfort a frightened little animal. She stroked the scars that formed thin weals on her husband's arms, kissed him and their tongues entwined. She did not say a word, but he guessed there must be a smile when, propped up on her elbow, she looked deep into the eyes of her man.

When he was a child in Chennai, Ranji had spent long hours by the river. He went there to swim, but also to watch the water hyacinths drifting on the surface, helplessly swept along by the current. And he wondered if they arrived somewhere, someday, and finding it good, stayed at that place forever.

Why did this memory come back to him that night? Maybe because he identified his journey from the banks of the Adyar with the slow migration of the hyacinths. A long roaming westwards into the unknown had brought him here, carried by the flood of hope, to this palace of palms and mud that housed his princess. Here he had put down roots, and fate had confirmed the validity of his choice. At that moment, he wouldn't have exchanged his situation for any other in the world.

The following day, when Surya came back from the school in the afternoon, Ranji asked her to reread, for the umpteenth time, the letter from his son and stopped her after the sentence about *'Birla Cement'* whose driver *'was supposed to visit Radapakkam.'* He would have bet he was driving with tyres like his.

"Tonight I will dictate to you a letter," he said, kissing his daughter.

Chapter 14
The Past is Another Country

Sometimes, something so unthinkable happens that we wonder again, a long time afterwards, if we didn't in fact dream it.

On the bus, packed with women and young children, there were only four men, and that included the driver. The other three must have been able to free themselves from their work for the pilgrimage to Shiva organised by the *panchayat* – the town council – of Puttur. Ashok was one of these three.

Meena had been shocked to see him get on the bus instead of Puna his wife, who she knew was supposed to be joining the trip. Then worry overtook her at seeing him advance confidently towards the back of the bus where she sat, and finally, anguish seized her as she sensed his musky aroma as he prepared to take the place next to her. The idea of having to travel pressed against the seducer, with his thick hands and bulging stomach plunged her into the depths of embarrassment. He bowed to her, smiling.

"Is Puna not coming?" she asked, her voice slurred with emotion.

"Ah no! Unfortunately she had to leave urgently to go to Mumbai. Her mother is not well…so I jumped at the chance!" Thus spoke Ashok, baring his golden teeth in a show of undisguised pleasure.

All seats on the bus had been taken and Meena saw no means of escape. Asking to change with anyone else would have been insulting to Ashok and would certainly have led to gossip. Despite his harassment of her, Ashok had been generous in recommending Santosh and it was thanks to him that her son now had a real job. She was still grateful for that.

But, feeling her neighbour's thigh pressing insistently against hers, she could only endure this contact by praying that the journey would not last too long. Obviously the brick-maker respected to the letter Article 17 of the Constitution: *Untouchability is abolished and its practice in any form is prohibited.* She chose not to react, but to hide her face in the loose edge of her sari and turned away from her neighbour to look out of the window, doing her best to ignore him.

However, that pest Indra, who was sitting two rows in front of them, then began her favourite pastime of making veiled allusions. Meena could see the small curvaceous woman in the reflection in the window. Ever since she had come upon Ashok paying assiduous court to Meena to the point of forgetting his cargo of bricks, Indra had played to the gallery when she was around: never actually naming Meena but dropping heavy hints, entertaining the others with her barbed teasing. Now Meena cowered down in her seat like a cat. She wanted only to disappear, to be invisible, to be dull and ugly, but the other woman was throwing out those little quips, punctuated by the laughter of her companions.

And the fat pig sitting next to her could also hear and would revel in the role of conqueror that cunning Indra was bestowing on him. Not wishing to raise her eyes, she kept her face expressionless, as do the Bhagavata dancers so beautifully, but then Ashok's voice broke in on her composure. Unable to avoid turning to face him now, she saw clearly in his eyes that glint of desire which gave away his thoughts, even as his hand was holding out a plastic bottle to her.

"I have brought with me water from the Himalayas, two mangoes, sandwiches and *pani puri*. We can share them!"

Meena did not answer. Her eyes were now firmly fixed on the seat back in front of her and what was left of the peeling paint scratched away before by millions of fingers. She wondered what she should do. Could this situation possibly have been engineered by Ashok, with the express purpose of being seated next to her? Had an evil demon decided to turn this pilgrimage into a trial to test her fidelity? Should she refuse to take anything, or was it better to accept? Would this risk creating the appearance of friendship, something that she wanted to avoid at all costs?

"Come on Meena! Just accept my offer. I am making it in good faith."

Ashok had taken out of the plastic bag on his lap a pungent doughnut stuffed with spicy vegetables, and he was offering it to Meena with his big hairy hand.

She took the doughnut, taking care to avoid touching his huge hand, praying to Ganesh, who removes obstacles, to give her the strength to resist any other proposal. But her heart was pounding and the jarring of the bus from the potholes had nothing to do with it. She whispered a 'thank you,' ate the doughnut quickly, pulled back into place the *pullu* of her sari to hide her face, then settled down again burrowed within its folds.

While Ashok sat beside her eating noisily, she let her eyes wander to the passing verges of the road – all much like each other. Pedestrians, rubbish, ox carts, *khetis*...When the bus stopped, hemmed in on all sides by traffic, Meena noticed bats, upside down, hanging from the branches of a tree like hundreds of black lanterns. She wondered as to the meaning of this omen, anxious to understand its sense, because despite everything that repulsed her in her neighbour, she still felt an attraction that was beyond her control. Distraught, she tried to sleep, but failing to do so, she pretended to have fallen asleep.

With sixty rupees taken from her own money, she had signed up for this trip. She wanted so much from Shiva! A visit from Santosh. Protection for the cabin during the fast approaching monsoon season. For Ranji to thrive by selling his tyre. These were what she planned to ask for in her prayers when she had handed over to the priest her small offering of coconut sprinkled with turmeric. Now she would add to this list her liberation from the satanic grip that Ashok seemed to have over her.

She would beg the god to reveal to her how best to loosen the stranglehold that gripped her heart in the presence of Ashok. To emerge from this confusion, this mixture of attraction and repulsion that she didn't seem able to control. The similarity to Ranji's obsession with his tyre seemed like the work of a demon. The round black shape, colour of the goddess Kali whose misdeeds were well known. Black as the grimacing bats, black as the night the monsoon had killed the goat, black as her thoughts.

The shameless courting of this man whose insistent pressure she felt against her thigh could only be yet one more curse added to her account. Not enough *puja*, gifts too insignificant, the gods were insistent on more evidence of devotion. They had sent a demon in the guise of the evil Ashok, and in order to resist him, Meena had to undertake some kind of purifying task though she knew not what it would be. And not finding it out, for a *dalit* like her, would certainly jeopardise a favourable reincarnation.

Despite the churning of these thoughts in her head, Meena did fall asleep, and this without first tasting the snacks or drinking the water from the Himalayas. And her dreams took over from the reality.

She saw again the kindly gentleman from her trip to the post office reading the *Times of India*, and, miraculously, she also understood what was written! A full page picture of her, with the generous body of Parvati, dancing with Shiva, basking in the tender gaze of Ranji, who, wreathed with flower necklaces, appeared as the leader of the BJP! Just like the President of the Republic, also an untouchable, her husband had become a leading man in the nation! Written in pretty characters similar to those made by Surya in her school notebooks, the text described how the sale of a tyre had triggered an avalanche of beneficial things, culminating in fame and the election of her husband to lead the fight against corruption. Just then, a humming sound engulfed Meena's head, and a snake emerged from a pile of wood, dancing as if stimulated by the smell of musky sandalwood. It swayed, jolting, jerking, and stood up in the left hand of Shiva. A curse was unfolding in accordance with the will of the gods, sweeping aside any grasp on reality.

The rocking of the seat which evoked the coming and going of waves, seemed to carry Meena over the surface of a vast ocean, rippled by the wind, and she was sailing towards unknown but clearly delightful shores in the company of this voluptuous snake. Her body was crumbling like sand while the spices and aromas of frangipani burst like droplets around them.

Detached from her body, like a piece of driftwood tossed on a sea of black ink, her spirit escaped, finally free from anxieties. She moved at will in this paradise, where infinite consorts and polymorphic avatars of familiar gods formed a merry band, welcoming their new princess with the sound of harps and tambourines. Flower blossoms, giant margosa whose leaves evoked thousands of green butterflies, sandalwood and lavatera, stems covered with purple flowers, bowed like suitors towards the multi-coloured arc of a rainbow.

And there on high, squatting on a ray of the arc, was pensive Ranji high above the clouds, contemplating the forlorn body of his wife at the back of a bus crowded with gossips and slanderers, her cherished body a pitiful victim to the weaknesses of passion.

In the noisy bus, stinking of sweat and burnt diesel, Meena had reached her nirvana, the state of abandonment, that absolute detachment from real life events that some strive to achieve during their whole lives aided by drugs or asceticism. She had found it just by the strength of her character, finding the antidote to her impulses in the folding inwards of herself, repelling the reality of the advances born from her own anguish. By giving free rein to her imagination, she could face real life now without fear of falling like a stone from this wonderful paradise. Unfortunately, a sudden braking brought her out of her reverie with a start, and she fell forward against the iron back of the seat in front of her.

She shot a frightened glance towards her neighbour. But Ashok was asleep, hands clasped together, head collapsed on his chest. The sight of him, reminded her of her father's version of the story of Kovalan that he had told her, that day when, frightened by what was happening to her, she discovered that she had become a woman.

It happened long ago, at the time of the Great Empire, in the era of the three kingdoms of Chola, Chera and Pandya. When the splendour of the Chola rulers was equalled only by their power and their immense territory connecting the Ganges and the Cauvery river. He told her how a fickle merchant named Kovalan, traveling in the kingdom, fell in love with Madhavi, a beautiful dancer. Pretty as a champaka flower, graceful as a wild orchid, she smelled of sandalwood and poppy seeds and danced like a queen. Forgetting his wife Kannagi, who, far away, was tending to their home and family in an exemplary fashion, the frivolous merchant had no qualms in conquering the heart of the beauty and in getting his way with her. He earned a living by trading and Madhavi's help in this was certainly significant because, to please this gorgeous woman, customers flocked to buy and good fortune led to more good fortune for him. In his anxiety to please Madhavi though he spent his whole fortune on her and was soon penniless.

So Kovalan reluctantly left this beautiful woman and returned to his home town and to his adoring wife Kannagi, who delighted in welcoming him home. Devoted as ever, she refused to believe the rumours she heard that he had been anything other than a loving faithful husband to her while away. To help him get back on his feet Kannagi gave him her valuable anklet to sell – one of a pair that had been made. It was a heavy bangle of gold and silver carved in such an intricate way that it seemed evident only queens and goddesses would wear something like this. Ignoble Kovalan accepted her gift and took it to the market with him to sell; but this anklet was so expensive and so rare that when it was seen he was immediately suspected of having obtained it fraudulently.

The Queen of Chola had owned an identical bangle, a gift from her husband, but it had been stolen from her. The king was informed of this strange coincidence and recognizing the anklet, he ordered the merchant to be beheaded without further ado and gave the piece of jewellery to the Queen.

Now Kannagi, the merchant's wife, had limitless faith in her husband. Whatever the reality of the facts seemed to show, she was absolutely convinced that her husband was faithful to her and loved her more than anything in the world. She was far from suspecting that this model of virtue could ever have betrayed her love, and her anger was directed only towards the king. She pondered long and hard on her vengeance against him, eventually settling on setting fire to Madurai, the capital of the Chola kingdom, and then fleeing to Chera where she committed suicide, in order to join her beloved Kovalan.

No longer fearful of meeting his eyes, Meena turned her head to look steadily at Ashok-Kovalan. To her he appeared even more ignoble, collapsed like a monkey on its belly.

She looked long and hard at her bronzed arms and at the bracelets decorated with cheap beads adorning her wrist. She held out her leg and studied the thin ring of silver, which must have been her most precious piece of jewellery. No gold or engraving embellished this gift from Ranji, only boundless love.

Recalling the story of Kovalan as told to her by her father, brought back to mind other memories of her family. That had all lived together in the Chettinad district, Meena, her three younger sisters and her two older brothers who worked in the rice fields. Her mother was a domestic servant in the big house of a rich Chettiar man called Joygopal Rao, and her father was a herdsman in charge of his cattle. They were allocated a room in the servants' quarters, close to the huge house. The room was tiny for eight people, and they were very poor, but on the whole, they were content. In the evenings, after work was finished, they sat in the twilight around their father while he told them the stories he had learnt from his own father.

She remembered when Ranji had arrived at the house and had been hired by Mr Rao to work in the fields. She had liked the look of this man but she had no idea, at that moment, he would be the man her parents would choose for her. Having asked in their prayers for advice from Prajapati, the god of marriage, they learnt from the priest that Meena's husband would be a man coming from the East. What a surprise it had been when she had seen him the day of their marriage and recognised him! And it was some years later, forced out of their home by the encroaching construction work, that they had decided to go their own way with the children. And driving with them the remaining goats from the dowry, they had set off to the West.

She smiled, her mind finally serene. The gods would always listen to the wishes of a pure soul.

CHAPTER 15
FAR FROM HOME

More than seven months had passed since Santosh had left his home at the side of the Radapakkam road. The young man, whose horizons had until then been confined to the village school, was now familiar with a distant city, had a regular job and was living with strangers. Carried as if by the wings of an angel in a fable, he felt he had landed in a new world. Now he had a completely new life, daily making new discoveries, and all made easier by his close friendship with Abi and Chan which worked so well, despite their differences in character. All three were from the lowest classes, that section of the population uniformly poor, ever present although not openly acknowledged, long condemned to survive in the service of others. Each had experienced poverty and suffering, the misery that teaches more than success or wealth, and each measured in his own way the not inconsiderable accomplishment of having become an employee of *Srivati & Co.*

For all three, the mere fact of having been hired by the company, when hundreds of others would have liked to be in their place, was a huge personal success, even a gift from the gods. This was how Santosh thought of it. Having been raised in a family in which everything they came by stemmed from their own effort, he considered that his parents had put in enough hard work, and that, somehow, it was natural that the gods were now compensating him. He was worthy of the honour, and he was certainly grateful for it, but he also behaved as if everything that was happening to him was natural, as if it had been inscribed on an invisible charter. This certainty gave him in those early days great assurance, a self-confidence that, eventually, would be decisive in his job.

Chan had an amazing physical strength and showed that passivity to events that is common in Indians of low birth. He demonstrated a kind of fatalism that derived as much from an acceptance of the conditions of his existence as the lack of any real means to escape from them. This stolid calm made him an agreeable companion who created no conflict. Although older than Santosh and having been in the business quite a few months longer, he had shown no resentment when the younger man had been preferred over him as deputy to Mr Jaigin. Chan accepted things without trying to influence them in any way. In many ways, his way of behaving, this lack of interest in competition, this docile submission, made him an easy roommate.

When they were deciding how they would organize themselves, the three boys all agreed that Abi should take the bed that his uncle had used in the room. Santosh had his eye on the place on the terrace but only as long as Chan had no objection. A tin roof sheltered the terrace from rain, and at night the breeze made it cooler than the room where the ceiling fan was permanently out of use. Chan agreed without hesitation, provided that he was able to store there his most valuable possession: his bicycle. He had a taciturn and serious face, often closed as if ruminating on his thoughts, or perhaps on an unmentionable secret. Chan was the only one of the three originally from the suburbs of Thanjavur. He had left his family for obscure reasons that he clearly did not wish to discuss, and the other boys, as if by agreement, did not pry. He slept the first day on a mat on the floor of the room, but the next day, he climbed the four floors with a *charpoi* in several pieces which he had somehow managed to carry there on his bicycle. He assembled it as well as he could and then placed it in between the door and the white wooden cabinet where everyone kept their few clothes. Chan, although a little slow in some ways, was gifted with a common sense that proved very useful to their little community. He managed to equip the place with a clay brazier to cook their food, some dishes and even assorted cutlery, and all without asking for any financial contribution from the other two. Santosh did ask himself how Chan came by these treasures but, sensing the boy's deep reluctance to reveal their provenance, decided to accept the contributions to the household with no awkward questions asked. Chan suggested that everyone should be responsible, in turn, for buying and preparing their evening meal for a week. They all found that a good idea.

Abi was of a very different nature. Quite tall and slim, he had a ready smile and his white teeth, like the whites of his eyes, permanently lit up his baby face with its very dark complexion. He took great care of his abundant hair, looking like shiny-black lacquer, which he wore in the style of a motorcycle helmet hugging his head. Extrovert, and constantly talking, mostly about girls, who undoubtedly represented for him the most interesting and mysterious thing in life, he often used his sense of humour to get his own way. Like Santosh, and unlike Chan, he had been educated though he seemed to have left school with only a rudimentary grasp of vocabulary. He had though an unshakeable conviction that he knew enough to get by, and it was this confidence in his own abilities that had led to his being hired. He too had acquired strength and the muscles to match from his previous work extracting sand from the river. He hit it off with Santosh immediately when they met in the queue.

Santosh positioned his mat close to the wall that enclosed the terrace and was happy to claim this open space where the three had their meals. He lay squeezed in close to the rickety table where they sat to eat their evening meal, and also right next to Chan's bicycle, but at any time he could stand up and lean on the balustrade, breathing in the warm air rising from the street. Sometimes spicy scents from the lower floors tickled his taste buds. More rarely he caught the fragrance of jasmine or rose, giving the illusion of a nearby garden. It enchanted him to contemplate, under the blue night, the crooked roofs of surrounding houses, imagining the lives of the people hidden underneath them. Here and there, on a roof terrace, a woman hung out her linen. Saris forming large colourful flags waved gently in the breeze.

Above this tangle of roofs and terraces, like a giant finger pointing to the sky, rose the massive conical silhouette of the *vimana* of the temple dedicated to Shiva. People came from all over India to pray there, and from all around the world just to marvel at this masterpiece of Dravidian architecture. Compared to the hut where he grew up, with its limited horizons and the ceaseless din of the road, the situation in his gazebo under the stars offered a multitude of points of interest. Up here he had the sense that he, the son of a poor *harijan*, dominated the world! This feeling produced in Santosh not so much pride as a sense of legitimate entitlement.

Those first months, he was often to be found there, leaning on the balustrade while the others slept, his head full of images which jumbled the present and the past. His harassed father depositing his bundle at the foot of the banyan. The proud figure of his mother leaving for the well with her jars, her face sombre but never complaining. Himself, waiting for the bus to go to school with Surya. While other children similarly badly off had no other choice but to assist their parents, Santosh and his sister were still studying because Ranji and Meena wanted them to have a better future. He was fully aware of the sacrifices that had been made for him. He remembered fondly impromptu cricket matches in the Rajah's field, using a branch shaped like a bat. The precious string ball wrapped in cloth flying from time to time deep into the thickets. Recovering it then turned the match partly into a treasure hunt.

He wondered about his friends back in the village and pondered on the great distance which now separated him from them. What were they doing now? He felt a strange melancholy when evoking those memories, as though in recklessly abandoning that miserable life, he had also lost a sure and certain happiness: the joy of living in a family surrounded by love. And he missed it. But with surprising maturity for his age, Santosh felt that the sadness of living at this great distance from his loved ones was worthwhile. He spent very little, gave up a third of his earnings for his living conditions, put aside some bank notes to send to his parents, and saved others to fulfil his own dreams.

Santosh had discovered an old Royal Enfield catalogue and secretly dreamed of one day being able to buy a motorcycle. He could just imagine arriving in Puttur on a Bullet 125 Classic, and could see clearly in his mind's eye the expression on his father's face. Truly it cost a fortune, but he was saving as carefully as his father, and the dream could become a reality. The gods seemed well disposed towards him.

He was endlessly grateful for his relationship with his boss. Jaigin was probably reliving through him, his own experiences. Served by his undoubted intelligence and by his sheer will to get on, he had been freed from any predestination. In a sense, you could say he embodied the hopes of a new generation – one that rejected the weight of tradition and forged its own future by using its own abilities. Seventy years after independence, a new India had been born, where everything now seemed possible. Jaigin took Santosh under his wing, like an older brother, and entrusted him with more and more administrative tasks. He sometimes shared more personal things with the younger man too, telling him about the birth of his child, or about his dear wife who prepared his daily lunch box. He often invited Santosh to share this with him, a clear sign of friendship and even affection. He started to tell Santosh stories of one of his sisters, who, with a troupe of *bharatanatyam* dancers was experiencing great success in Chennai with the *kuchipudi* plate dance.

These confidences acted as a soothing balm for the soul of the young man. And now he had also been given access to the computer to place orders. At school in Puttur, the final year students had been taught how to use the keyboard on an old IBM, and Santosh had quickly understood the value of this machine. Jaigin spent time teaching him about the software used by *Srivati* in the gatehouse that served as his office. Then, one day, he told him his access code and gave him instructions on how to place the orders.

Working mostly inside the building, Santosh himself was not too affected by the dry season and the 90°F temperature, but Abi and Chan, who still worked in the courtyard under the scorching sun, did begin to envy their friend. Although the interior of the depot was also as hot as a furnace, Santosh was allowed to make use of the room that was used to meet suppliers, and there he could enjoy the cooling effect of his benefactor's fan. Whenever possible, he arranged for his friends to join him there, warning them not to abuse the privilege. Jaigin had certainly spotted what was going on but pretended to notice nothing until the day Abi had the audacity to sit in the boss's chair, which nearly cost him his job.

Santosh's reputation for being resourceful, but also the attraction of the cooling fan, encouraged the employees to consult him when a delivery arrived or a delicate problem arose. In short, the young *dalit* was one of the "promising talents," as Jaigin told him one midday over a shared lunch of two doughnuts with green peppers.

Only one thing threatened to disturb his pleasure in this remarkable trajectory from abject poverty to his present fortunate situation: he hated to admit it, even to himself, but he had started to distrust Chan. Always quiet, verging on taciturn, Chan had been a valued friend and trusted colleague until the time Santosh returned to the office after being called to attend to one of the deliveries and found him waiting just inside the door of the room to speak to him. Though never expressly forbidden from entering the room alone he had never expected that Chan would assume this privilege. Santosh's start of surprise to find the young man there alone and then the obvious annoyance seen on his face at this untoward situation was clear to Chan. He blushed deep red, blurted out his message and hurried out. It was not mentioned again but something between them had undoubtedly changed. Chan seemed even more closed, even sullen at times.

Worse was to come when some weeks later Jaigin came to collect his jacket which earlier in the day he had left in the room where Santosh worked. He was surprised to see Jaigin anxiously searching through his jacket pockets and then swear aloud – a formerly unthinkable reaction from the older man.

"Did anyone come in here Santosh?" he asked. "I'm missing a banknote – 500 rupees – I know I had it in my pocket this morning. I shouldn't have left it in here but......"

Santosh's thoughts flew to Chan and the time he had found him in the room. Now it was his turn to blush as he hastened to assure his boss that he had seen no-one enter the office. Although this was true a nagging doubt hung over him. Was the time he had found his coworker there the only time Chan had entered the room alone, or was this his habit? Could Chan possibly have taken Jaigin's money? Then an even more horrifying thought crossed his mind. Might Jaigin think Santosh himself had taken the note? Surely not! Reading on the younger man's face something of his inner turmoil Jaigin attempted to lighten the mood:

"Don't worry Santosh. It probably fell out of my pocket somewhere. It's my fault – I should be more careful."

But the seed of doubt was planted now and try as he might Santosh could not shake it off. He vowed to watch Chan more closely in the future.

His other companion Abi had quickly noticed a girl, Puthu, who with her brother Deepan and their parents, lived below them on the second floor. She was fifteen, with long braids and laughing eyes. They crossed on the stairs as she went to school and Abi had made her laugh with his jokes. These two were now in love, and Santosh was amused by their discreet little game. Girls did not really interest him. He had always found them incomprehensible and capricious. Even Surya, he felt, used her youth and her feminine wiles to get things he would never dare to ask for from his parents. Although now that she was so far away, he missed his little sister much more than he had expected to.

On days off, Abi took Puthu to the cinema or they just strolled along the river, and Chan left his co-tenants saying he was going to visit one of his many brothers or sisters. Santosh regretted that his own family were not a typical Indian family. He had complained about this to his mother, when at the age of ten he was still the only boy in the family, and discovered from her about "family planning". A method according to Meena to avoid poor people having too many mouths to feed. When her belly had rounded Santosh had been hoping for a little brother, and the birth of Surya was initially a disappointment, although it then became a happiness even before she became the little treasure she was now.

On those days then, with Abi and Chan away, Santosh was alone. He took the opportunity to do his laundry and also did the shopping for their little household. He went to the temple regularly to thank the gods for their kindness towards him, but his favourite pastime was to take a solitary stroll through the streets overflowing with every kind of activity, observing the tourists who wandered with their cameras in small groups towards the great temple. Europeans with their white skin in their short trousers, blonde women with blue eyes, the Japanese with their short legs: all huddled behind their guides, and mingled with the motley crowd. You would never see something like this in Puttur. It gave the city a special atmosphere, vibrant and peaceful at the same time, filled with scents and colours, a different sensory experience to that of the countryside. How he would have liked to have a mobile phone, to speak to his parents as he knew did more and more people who lived away from their families, but what use would that have been to him anyway since his parents did not have one? He had received no reply to his letter. This did not unduly surprise or worry him. He only hoped that everyone was okay.

Entrusting his first missive to a *Birla* delivery man he thought he had chosen the safest way to get it delivered, by hand, to his parents, but the guy had died in an accident. Discovering this some time later, he wrote again, but he had worried as he slipped the three hundred rupees saved for them into this second letter. Having never used the mail system before, he feared that it could also be lost, but he took the risk. At the same time, he took advantage of the free time he had to learn about the prices and specifications of second hand motorcycles.

The north wind brought the first black clouds warning of the winter monsoon. And then the rains came. All knew that they could be devastating. At the *Srivati* company they began to move the most moisture-sensitive materials under cover. Chan was carrying bags of plaster and cement all day long and came home exhausted and grumpy at night. Abi and other employees covered the timber carefully with tarpaulins. They filled sandbags to protect the site from the flood water because, according to Mr Paniandy, it could be turned into something resembling a lake in less than a day.

One evening he came home from work, and finally found a sealed envelope slipped under the door. Immediately he recognized his sister's handwriting. His heart began to beat faster. He was so eager to know its contents, he nearly tore it in his haste to open the envelope.

Reassured at last about the fate of his last letter and the money, he then discovered the existence of the tyre. At first, he wanted to laugh, as much at the way Surya told the story as by the imbecility of the driver liable for that loss. He himself checked the deliveries from dozens of trucks arriving at the warehouse and often found things missing, so he had no illusions about the seriousness of some carriers. Most often, the missing bag of cement appeared in the cab, strangely enough! And one could assume that the few missing bricks from a pallet had not evaporated during the ride!

He would have liked to have more news of his family, but the letter spoke only of this huge tyre his father was so obviously desperate to sell. He imagined the situation and began to look into the issue. Maybe Jaigin would have an idea.

He would talk to him.

CHAPTER 16
THE NEGOTIATION

B ack in the village, the months passed, their rhythm punctuated by festivals – religious and otherwise. Almost
every month offered an opportunity for some kind of obser-
vance: the celebration of Vishnu, Banashankari, Carnatic
music festival, Pooram, Aradhana, the festival of chariots,
Ararat festival, the snake-boat race of Kottayam... Those
who could attend, making use of all possible means of transport, reported back on the joyful enthusiasm of those gathered together to those back at home who were not able to
go due to lack of funds.

The poorest were content to walk to local festivals
organized in Puttur by political parties, anniversaries of
independence or other political-religious events. Legions
of flags, banners and pennants adorned the crumbling
facades of houses, and up above, attached by string to tele-
graph poles, speakers broadcast distorted popular music
interspersed with slogans in praise of the MP, the President
of the Republic, or the Governor.

These events were huge festivals which mingled parades,
folklore, and social occasions with religious devotion where
you could buy balloons or plastic trumpets, beads, sandalwood balls or garlands of flowers. You returned home after

these fiestas a few rupees poorer but enriched by having taken part in a vibrant community event and happy perhaps to have caught up with a lost or forgotten friend.

Meanwhile, at the hut, suspended by its coconut hemp rope, the tyre was still waiting to be claimed by its buyer.

Although he had done his best at the nearby petrol station, and then tried to get some result from the local bus and taxi drivers, all Sharad Sarin's attempts had drawn a blank. Now Ranji could only curse Sarin, who seemed to have lost all interest in their potential deal. And having waited in vain for a response to his letter to Santosh, Ranji decided that he himself would go to Puttur to see the neighbour of the ironworker who made agricultural tools.

This craftsman made baskets from old tyres by cutting them with shears into three sections. His magical operation consisted of turning them inside out and thus the concave became convex. He had only to rivet two handles in place and the resulting container was practically indestructible.

The baskets of this surgeon of last resort were piled up in front of the shop. Heartsick, Ranji asked him how much he might buy his tyre for. The frank answer was that it was too big and therefore more difficult to cut, but the man consented to give him a hundred rupees after a long negotiation. A nice sum for a swing, but in no way commensurate with the hopes which had been raised by the estimate of the sage. However, the basket maker was a kind man and advised him to canvass traders working in the automotive sector. There was one he said, who rather grandly termed himself "Official Distributor" on the outskirts of the city. Ranji set off to find him.

Stepping over the mechanical parts that littered the front of the store, on a dirt floor soaked with motor oil, Ranji went directly to talk to the boss. Having now been thrust into the situation of interacting with all kinds of people, he had rehearsed his speech. The man wore glasses and an overall which might well have been blue one day but whose colour now blended in perfectly with his environment – black, iron, rusty. He took his time in finishing his conversation on the phone, finally placed his mobile phone on a bench between a connecting rod and a piston in particularly poor shape, and then turned his attention to Ranji.

For the very first time, Ranji felt that he had awakened some real interest. The official distributor made him confirm several times that the tyre really was new, and Ranji having insisted that it had never been used, he seemed satisfied. The mechanic's cousin knew of a used tyre dealer: he would talk to him.

The broker took some time to find his way to the hut. He arrived from Tiruchirappalli one Sunday morning early in September, the day of Janmashtami, on a black Honda motorcycle, turned rusty red by the laterite dust. He was the person suggested by the "Official Distributor" of Puttur.

Ranji was criss-crossing the dry palms on the roof of the hut to form an additional covering before the first rains began because the air had felt heavy for the last few days. Surya and her friends were laughing and splashing each other using a bowl they had found in a ditch. It was very hot and the cow was lying in the shade of the banyan.

Meena was grilling the last of the cashews, beside the road, in a halo of grey smoke and ashes. When she realized that under the amber dust, the motorcycle man was dressed from head to toe in black, a shiver ran through her. Black: the colour of the hanging bats by the road, and the colour of that damn unsaleable tyre! She had become convinced that black meant bad luck.

Once his machine was secured on its stand the man approached Ranji, wiping the dust from his face with the back of his hand. Straightaway he saw the tyre hanging from its branch.

"They told me you had a new tyre for sale," said the man in Tamil, but with a strong northern accent.

Ranji was giving the impression of someone with a lot to do, and having carefully completed his task, arranging a palm just so in order to properly fill a gap, he raised his head to look at the newcomer. He noted how youthful he looked, and the confidence with which he addressed him without even having introduced himself. He took in the clothes of a city dweller, noted the colour of his skin, his smooth forehead, his eyes reddened by the wind, and finally the heat from the bike that was still cooling down. A powerful model. The man had tried to conceal his youth with a thin, neatly trimmed beard. He had obviously come a long way to visit him. Ranji tried to calm the excitement that leapt in his heart.

"Yes, here it is," he said, pointing to his prized possession. "My name is Ranji. Did the distributor from Puttur send you?"

"One of his family, yes. My name is Sudarshan Jagadisha Singh, I am Punjabi. They call me Mr Singh."

"And you've come from the Punjab?" Ranji was surprised as the last geography lesson from Surya had given him the idea that this state was thousands of kilometres away.

"No!" laughed Mr Singh, "I live in Chennai. It's far enough away already! But I was told about a new tyre!"

"It is new," insisted Ranji going to fetch the plastic film packaging with the yellow and blue label preserved like a treasure for safety in the hut.

"It doesn't look like it, from what I can see."

"I can assure you it is! Look at the packaging. I'll get it down for you to take a closer look."

Ranji hurried to release the tyre from where it hung and it fell to the ground in front of the buyer in a cloud of fine flour-like dust.

"It is a 22.5 – that diameter of the rim is rare," said the broker after a quick look at the tyre.

"What is rare is expensive," retorted Ranji passing over the meaning of the word rim.

"What is rare is not easy to sell," objected the broker.

While examining the sidewalls and tread, he stroked his beard in a thoughtful way.

"How much do you want for it?"

"Seven thousand rupees," interjected Ranji, surprising himself by speaking aloud the price he had dreamed of.

The young man laughed, straightening up.

"I understand now why you haven't sold it yet! It is not worth more than a thousand. Of course, living out here it must be difficult for you to know the true value of things," he added, surveying with a glance this down-at-heel area to which his work had brought him.

Although he was used to visiting poor places to come across tyres mostly good for nothing except crushing, never before had he gone to a hut of palms to negotiate the purchase of a new tyre, and all the evidence indicated that this tyre was new and in perfect condition. And what a tyre! This novel situation was comical: a barefoot man selling a brand new tyre to a broker of used tyres! The very opposite of the norm, but no reason why a good deal should prove impossible to strike.

"A thousand rupees," he said again. "Believe me, that's a good price! Don't forget my friend, I can't carry it on my bike. I have to consider the transport," the young man remarked, laughing.

For Ranji a thousand rupees was without doubt a nice sum in absolute terms. More than a month's salary from the Rajah, and ten times the offer of the basket maker. But it was so far from the estimate given by the *sadhu* that he in his turn laughed too.

"I'm afraid that you have had a wasted journey," he said, making as if to go back to his palms.

At that moment, Surya appeared as if by magic. She was wearing her sky-blue school dress despite the ban on this from her mother who wanted it to stay immaculate. She was so proud to show it off to everyone that she was continually being scolded for not changing out of it after school. And now here she was with her dress wet and hair dripping. But Meena surmised that this was not the right time to express her anger.

"Look what I've been given," announced Surya happily.

She showed two small cat fish in her hands.

"Who gave them to you?" Meena asked sharply.

"Some boys who were playing with us."

Suddenly, seeing the rope hanging from the banyan like a dead vine and the tyre, also lying as if dead in front of the stranger, she screamed.

"Why have you destroyed my swing?"

Meena deftly grabbed the arm of her daughter and hurried her inside the hut. Controlling the urge to slap her, she explained that it is not *her* swing but the property of her father and that the bearded gentleman had come to buy the tyre. The high spirits of Surya were eclipsed, blown out like a candle flame, and she threw the fish down in a temper, devastated at the prospect of losing the only way she had to attract her friends to the *kheti*.

"Surya, stop messing about, pick up the fish this moment! One day the money from that tyre will enable your father to find you a good husband. You must not hinder the transaction. Do as I do, listen and say nothing, but first pick up those fish and rinse them under the water. We do not throw away food. Then put the lentils in to soak and go and fetch the cow."

Surya obeyed, wondering what her tyre could possibly have to do with a husband. However, she did remember that one day, one of the girls in the class above, had left school in tears. Rumour had it that she had gone away to be married. Frankly she would much prefer to have the tyre to swing on than to see it exchanged to get her a husband! She resolved to try to sabotage the negotiation in her own way.

While her mother was roasting some nuts taking care to be as unobtrusive as possible, and while the two men were deep in discussion under the banyan tree, Surya spent her time coming and going. She found any and every pretext to get closer to the stranger speaking with her father and to hear what they were saying.

"If you had offered me an 18.5 in this state, I'd have bought it from you immediately. And for a good price! I would have gone up to at least one thousand six hundred rupees, but for a tyre of this type, there is not much of a market. If I go up to one thousand five hundred I would be making a huge exception for you."

"People supposed to be experts tell me to accept no less than six thousand: I'm not sure there is much point discussing this any more; I'd be better off carrying on covering the roof with palms," retorted Ranji suiting his action to the words.

Meena, who was watching the scene out of the corner of her eye whilst stirring the nuts in their clay pot said nothing but rolled her eyes. To put an end to this story, she would sell this detested tyre at any price. She wavered between concern and admiration for the composure of her husband. His mastery of the large numbers amazed her. He, who normally dealt in *annas* and *naye paise*, seemed perfectly comfortable discussing thousands of rupees. Her instincts were that he was trying to achieve a figure of two thousand rupees, which was truly an extraordinary sum. Enough to buy not only a bicycle but perhaps a Chinese refrigerator, her secret dream. She waited for the next stage with ears eager and alert.

"Where shall I put the fish?" Surya shouted loud enough for everyone to hear. Her eyes sparkled as she toyed with her braids in a gesture of the best feminine coquetry. But no one answered.

Playing his role, Ranji had returned muttering to his palms, adopting a disinterested air. The broker inspected the inside of the tyre moving his hand along the walls. He was obviously looking for a hidden defect or something to justify a low offer.

"You can see the marks left by the rope here and there, it decreases the value. You should not have hung it up."

Without looking up and keeping himself busy Ranji replied.

"A few marks won't prevent it from carrying cement!"

"Well then? What's your best price?" asked the broker.

"I've told you...But as you have come a long way, five thousand and a can of coconut oil."

The broker did not get up and said nothing, which Ranji interpreted as a very encouraging sign. For a moment he thought he should have remained firm but his optimism was short-lived.

"You're not being reasonable about the price," said the broker, "for a product like this. "It is true that I have passed through many towns and burned a lot of fuel to get here, but fortunately I found other business because of your tyre... Come on, I'll go up to one thousand eight hundred." Unaccountably, at the same time as he announced his revised offer, his eyes left the tyre to take in the spectacle that Surya was making. The girl came and went, throwing teasing glances in his direction, flipping the lentils, kicking up the dust, singing louder than she should have, all in order to get herself noticed.

Meena was about to intervene to calm her down when she caught the look of the young man. There was a gentleness in his eyes and an interest in the little seductress who, without truly being aware of what she was doing, was providing a truly charming sight.

Ranji interrupted this glamour session with a question that surprised the young man:

"The tyres that you buy, is it you who sells them?"

"No, it's not me. We are four brothers, I am the broker, I buy what my brothers can sell. If you had suggested a 385 / R65 or even a 295 / R80, I would have been interested immediately, the 295, it is very suitable for tuk-tuks and for small carts also..."

"So you said, already," commented Ranji, affecting little interest.

Despite his air of confidence Ranji was hesitant as to what he should do. He had still heard nothing from Santosh since he wrote the letter asking for his help. So should he close the deal here and now, or push for a bit more? One thousand eight hundred rupees: it wasn't bad, but if this kind of tyre sold for up to seven thousand in the shops, as suggested by the *sadhu*, then he wanted to go on. But if he was to have any chance of achieving such a sale, with the only serious buyer who had shown up, he still had to make a huge effort.

"So? The fish, where shall I put them?" asked Surya again, feigning anger that no-one but the stranger seemed interested in her question.

"Four thousand, one gallon of oil and it is yours," said Ranji, daring this time to meet the eyes of the young man.

But Mr Singh's attention had moved away from the negotiation. He was visibly amused by Surya's antics and seemed entranced by the assurance of this little woman. Surya, the adored baby of the family, confident of her appeal, was growing up fast, and nowadays neither the father absorbed by his transaction, nor the mother focused on her home, was a match for her wilful personality. A good sign for the future, Ranji might have thought.

Meena's patience eventually snapped and she scolded her daughter in Malayalam so the man with the bike would not understand – Surya knew very well how to prepare the fish: putting them in the pan where the *ghee* sizzled, and she must cease immediately her antics which could jeopardise this difficult negotiation. Still smiling, the bearded young man reproached Ranji.

"You're a very hard case! I will offer you two thousand rupees and the can."

"No," said Ranji after a short time of reflection, "It is not enough. I cannot accept."

Two vertical furrows formed in the forehead of the man and his eyes changed their expression. He got up, muttering in a language unknown to Ranji, took a cell phone from his pocket and walked away tapping in numbers.

Ranji watched him. The left hand of the man held the phone against his ear, his arm, positioned in a triangle, did not move, as if welded in that position, while the other swept the air in strange gestures as strange sounds came from his mouth. The broker struck out in one direction, stopped and then set off again in the other. Seeing neither cars, nor trucks nor tuk-tuks pass, he seemed to be talking to the birds.

After a long moment, he closed his phone, slipped it into his pocket and turned back towards Ranji, but Meena, who was watching from her position below, while cracking her nuts at the same time, noticed that the eyes of the broker sought out their little daughter.

"Listen," said the young man to Ranji, "I cannot contact the only customer that might be interested in your tyre. He is a Christian and on Sundays he's at church. I'm going to Radapakkam to try to see whether we can do something with him. I can't promise anything. If I'm not back in a week, you have lost the deal."

With a sudden movement revealing her disappointment, Meena tipped out the small charred shells and swept away the remains of the fried fish onto the ground. The gesture was not lost on Ranji. The conviction that his tyre was worth much more than the last offer of the arguing broker had made him reluctant to accept even this significant amount. He read a rebuke like a flash of lightning in the eyes of his wife but he stood firm on his decision. The 'No,' peremptory and assured that he had dared to utter, felt like the revelation of unprecedented power. For the first time in his life, a man accustomed to bend to the wills of others had expressed his refusal. He hadn't gained the money, but he drew immense pride from this nevertheless.

"Well then, I must bid you perhaps goodbye. We have not done business today," said the broker in a final attempt as he started preparing to get on his bike. "It's really a shame because you have a very charming daughter!"

Ranji did not react, but Meena started as if struck by a brilliant idea.

"We have not even offered you a glass of tea, we fail in our duty of hospitality! I beg you *sahib* Singh, please agree to drink tea with us."

"Oh, of course," added Ranji now contrite. "Mr Singh, please do us the honour of staying for a while! Surya prepare the tea and bring three glasses!"

The bearded one readjusted his Honda onto its stand and sat down on a log that served as a seat in front of the *kheti*. It was without doubt a very poor place covered with its untidy palms!

They talked for an hour, about life, about the weather, about the banyan tree which seemed to murmur with the bustle of the birds, about the difficulties of life in the city, about the trade in used tyres, cashews and the future for children. Mr Singh had not been and was not married. Neither of them broached the two subjects which occupied them: the threshold of two thousand five hundred rupees that would have changed Ranji's mind, and the future of small Surya who would have made a very young but delectable wife. They talked until the flock of crows came to scrounge for the scraps from the hut.

The broker got to his feet without increasing his last offer and Meena shuddered once again because to her it seemed that since the pilgrimage to Srirangam, everything that drove, flew, or was seen as significant was black, just as was the motorcycle of this bearded one.

The Sikh thanked them for the *chai*, complimented Surya on her smile, hinted that he would return and then the bike disappeared into the distance with a thrumming drone. Even before Meena had a chance to tell him what she thought of his grotesque obstinacy, Ranji broke in.

"He isn't a Sikh, despite his beard, I'm sure he is a Christian. I saw their sign hanging round his neck. And I am equally sure that he is a *dalit*. He will come back…"

In this way he was trying to minimise his disappointment. It was only his pride that had prevented him from running behind the bike shouting out that he accepted the last offer. The terrible feeling of having missed his chance now bore down on him like a heavy stone. The bulky tyre was still lying there, abandoned in the dust, and his hands held no rupees.

He sat on his heels thoughtfully, his eyes far away and blank, and a long time passed with him barely registering the scolding of Meena.

Surya brought out the pan with the fish, humming happily. She had won the battle to keep *her* tyre!

"That was not a *sardar*, he had cut his hair," said Ranji thoughtfully as if this comment of no particular interest could detract attention from what now seemed a fiasco.

"Whatever! Your stubbornness cost us two thousand rupees! Bravo!"

"Many untouchables choose to become communists or Christians, because for them all men are equal," replied Ranji, pursuing his idea.

Ranji had heard about these departures from the centuries-old traditions that the authorities had condoned. Those *dalits* raised their heads and could also say "No," just as he had done so bravely.

"Modern s*ardar* or Christian, d*alit* or not, he was ready to buy your damn tyre! Tomorrow you could be riding your bicycle! Two thousand rupees, can you imagine!"

"Daylight robbery, yes!" said Ranji. "You'll see that I was right. If the *sadhu* told me the truth, and I see no reason for him to have lied to me, we shall see him again soon."

"He seemed nice," Surya said, just happy to have saved her swing.

That night, a sudden gust of wind shook the palms on the roof. This had not happened for months. The air grew heavy, the plumes of areca, perched at the top of their skinny trunks, fluttered in the clammy twilight like the heads of migratory birds. Rubbing against each other, the palms gave off their characteristic rustling sound like crumpled cardboard, and like the masts of ships heckled by the sea, the trunks began to sway. The signs of the monsoon were becoming clearer. In the hut the heat was becoming unbearable. Ranji left the *charpoi* to sleep outside and to enjoy the cooler air which dried the sweat on his body.

The glow of the kerosene lamp illuminated the tense face of Meena who was munching on a rounded green chili.

"You'll never get your bike," she stated, allowing her sentence to fall as sharply as the blade of a machete on a chopping block.

"He will come back," answered Ranji who had brought out the *rasgullah*, sweets made with milk from the cow to soothe the heat of the peppers.

The question of whether it was right or wrong to refuse was still swirling around in his mind, but the sweltering heat had softened his brain. He was incapable of rational judgment and clung desperately to the hope that the broker would return whilst claiming it vehemently as a certainty.

"He may come back," Meena said as if reading the thoughts of her husband, "But not for your tyre…"

"What for then?"

Meena motioned with a look towards Surya.

Ranji's eyes widened in surprise.

"Don't tell me, you…" he stopped, amazed at this suggestion of his wife.

"As usual, you noticed nothing. The antics of your daughter! The gaze of that young man…"

"Meena, surely you can't seriously think that! What is going through your mind?" Well, obviously there were still marriages of children despite the laws, but that his wife had been able to consider this left him speechless. He would not even broach the subject. One does not marry a girl, first in her class, who could study at college and become one day a civil servant, to a tyre buyer, quite possibly a swindler, or at the very least an uncooperative one!

"I noticed that the last nut sack is empty. So you have nothing to roast now?" Ranji commented.

"There, you have said it. Bad luck for your bike."

"It can wait another week. I have always walked. I can do so a little longer."

"Last night I had a dream," said Meena. "I did not know that the broker would come today. I saw all four of us, perched on the back of an elephant. Maybe it is a sign that our wishes will be granted. That Ganesh is interested in us! He may come back, but there has been too much black lately. You saw the colour of his motorcycle! That worries me."

Chapter 17
The Monsoon

The astrologer of Puttur took his time before unveiling his verdict to the *panshayat*, the town council, who had come to consult him. Feet firmly planted on a *swastika of* blue powder drawn on the ground, he was rolling coriander seeds round in a bronze bowl, turning it slowly around whilst chanting mantras known only to him. The small balls gave him valuable information, or at least that is what he claimed, and what the board members gathered around him believed. He silenced their murmurs with a gesture, and, in the silence that followed, listened to the sound of the wind, the birdsong, and sniffed at the aroma of salt which came from the south.

The only diviner in the region, and always called upon to predict the weather, he returned his fiery gaze to the round bowl, fully attentive to the pattern of the seeds. Then, suddenly, he raised his turbaned head towards the leader of the *panshayat*. A big gust of wind, which shook the dust which had accumulated on the leaves of trees over many months, accompanied his next statement. Praising Bhagavati who had entrusted this knowledge to him, he announced the imminent arrival of the monsoon.

Straightaway the council decided to equip a three wheeled motorcar with a loudspeaker, the usual way of advertising, and with a microphone go around the region warning the population. Everyone would therefore be able to make preparations for this radical change in the climate which, for two months, would transform the land into mud, the fields into lakes and the ditches into rivers.

Knowing that supplies would be badly disrupted by these conditions, Meena, like many others, went into town and came back laden with dried goods and tins of preserved food. Ranji in his turn, bought wax candles and filled the can with kerosene to cope with the frequent power cuts, whilst also making efforts to strengthen the structure of the hut with the famous bricks given by Ashok. As happened every year, the issue of the cow was aired. What should they do with her? Who could they entrust her to this time? Certainly not to their relative Arun, the eldest son of a distant cousin who lived in the hills of Kampbush, an area safe from flooding. The previous year, despite having the benefit of the plentiful supplies of milk taken from his lodger, the cousin treated the cow worse than a stray dog.

Helped by the fact that he was employed by the Rajah, and with the support of Sharad, who truth be told was a little embarrassed at not having succeeded in his mission as an intermediary, Ranji got permission for his cow to join his boss's herd during the rainy period. A guarantee of the fodder being offset against the milk taken from the beast, and the expectation of getting her back in better condition than was the case the previous year was more than enough to convince Ranji that this was the best possible scenario.

As for Ashok, he redeemed himself somewhat by offering to host the whole family at his place. The offer in itself was not especially exceptional. Coming usually from relatives, this kind of arrangement allowed the poor to escape calamity. But coming from Ashok the brick manufacturer, usually so haughty and contemptuous, the offer not only surprised Ranji but made him immediately suspicious. Such a gesture of magnanimity, on top of the bricks, could not be a disinterested one. He prevaricated.

No special bonds of affection bind us, I am already in his debt for what he did for Santosh, and then for the bricks, and I should be even more indebted by accepting shelter. What service will he expect in return? These were the issues he pondered.

He concluded first that the only explanation was to be found relating to what was most precious to him: his wife and daughter. The idea alone froze his blood. But upon further reflection, he decided he must be mistaken. A *kshatriya* would not even touch the hand of a *dalit*. He was getting fanciful! Could it be right to make his treasures suffer the cold, the damp and the discomfort, when they could be sleeping dry and sheltered in a real building? Vicash and his family took advantage of this roof every monsoon. And Surya would be delighted to be with her friend. But even if he was minded to accept Ashok's offer for them, he decided that he, in any case, would have to remain longer at the *kheti* to welcome Mr Singh when he came back with his rupees. The broker had not yet shown up but Ranji was convinced that this was just a temporary delay, a setback. No, it would certainly be better to wait for his return with the money.

Satisfied by his own justification he refused Ashok's proposal. But he thanked him warmly for the bricks with which he planned to build a small wall to protect the hut from potential flooding. That could happen if the water overflowed from the three small ditches that lined the road. The year before, the liquid mass accumulated in the Rajah's fields had crossed the dam of the second trench, washing around the roots of the bushes. The black wave had carried with it a multitude of rubbish which had caught in the thread roots of the banyan, creating a stinking mound near the hut, forming a dam, with pockets of stagnant and stinking water swarming with mosquitoes and snakes.

"Well, it is your right to refuse," retorted Ashok annoyed, "But you should think about your family. Remember last year! At least make sure they are safe!"

"Safe from what? Safe from you?" Ranji thought. His gaze was caught by Meena's posture. She was nestling her head in the *pullu* of her sari, looking at the chipped nail polish on her toenails, just as perplexed as her husband. Folded in on herself, wrapped in her sari like a laundry woman, she saw the black water that seeped into the hut and rose inexorably. It brought back to her mind the nightmare of that desolate landscape all around their sinking island the year before.

She knew she could not bear to relive again the waiting, the watching, wondering if they were to succumb to drowning, just like Vicash's son. She understood very well why Ranji hesitated, she was fearful herself at being in the same environment as Ashok, even if they would not be housed in the main house but in his warehouse.

Meena thought very carefully before saying anything. Her mind was teeming but she showed no obvious sign of her inner turmoil. She was beset by dark and terrible images of the flood, the slimy water in which they would be floundering, the hut turned inside out at night, the cry of the hyenas seeking out the corpses of drowned animals. And this scenario might, anyway, still be followed by their forced flight to the village where, in the courtyard, crowded together in destitution, would be the poor from the whole region. So, on the one hand, the abandonment of their home, but on the other, a safe roof, solid walls and dry soil.

Without knowing how to read the scriptures, Meena has an intuition for signs, for interpreting events, for identifying both bad omens and favourable signs, for she was sure that nothing happened in human life that was not dictated by a higher power. She knew that a demon had captured the soul of Ashok well before the pilgrimage to Srirangam, but that Shiva had given her the strength to resist the brick maker's indecent advances.

Perhaps, after all, like a good Hindu, Ashok was simply offering assistance to his brothers in religion, but even so she feared being seen as a chattel because of her lower caste. According to Puna, the *panshayat* planned to commandeer the school premises. If the water did rise further, Ranji and his family could take shelter there.

"You're right, Ranji, I don't want to accept the offer either," she finally said.

It ended there. For a time.

When the atmosphere became so damp that their clothes stayed wet all the time, and she felt on waking as though she was in a bath, Meena, without actually giving voice to her thoughts, began to change her mind. A dark and tortured mass invaded the clear sky that floated over the plains during the dry season. Like a mighty steamroller, the black clouds coming from the ocean advanced by rolling over on themselves, flattening everything that was in their way.

Sweat trickled from bodies. The trees lining the road were sweating too. Large drops fell from the leaves, but instead of bursting when touching the ground, they turned into dust balls. Then the sky was streaked by lightning and took on the colour of lead while the thick air seemed to support its weight. Compressed in this moist mass, humans struggled to move. Finally, the clouds burst and the rain fell, blurring the world, in a crash of doom.

Most exhausted pedestrians no longer wanted to, nor were able to walk. The water was beautiful, sacred and beneficial for the earth, but their legs, wobbly like sticks of liquorice, could carry them no further. They became stuck in the viscous mud that formed in the pathways. Dazed, people stood stranded under any shelter, dripping with warm water, waiting patiently for it to stop. But it did not stop.

Here and there, women could be seen sitting on a tree trunk or a low wall waiting for a hypothetical bus. They fanned themselves with twigs, the sweeping gesture indicating weariness with the rain falling in front of their impassive faces.

Some, eager to reach their homes, provisions on their heads as a pathetic protection, still fought to make progress against the gusts. From the hut, Ranji saw these ghostly figures soaked by the wash from the vehicles. Headlights lit, they ploughed mercilessly through the water, until the road turned into a river, and then this was no longer practical. Lethargy invaded their bodies, and on these oppressed people, the unleashed sky poured everything it had absorbed from the ocean over the year. It looked like it was expelling its whole brazen insolence against the excesses of the sun. The heat heavily laden with humidity became stifling, rain fell continuously, the water began to rise.

The palm roof showed its first signs of weakness. The water began to drip down on Meena and on Surya, clasped in her arms. Ranji, braving the elements, went out to try to repair the covering of palms. He came back in soaking wet but without having been able to improve the seal.

And still no Mr Singh.

The rain fell heavily throughout the night. Ranji did not close his eyes. With the second day proving identical to the first Ranji dug up the can of Pepsi and took out some money, then left the hut without saying where he was going. Meena thought he must be going to Ashok.

He returned at midday carrying on his back two corrugated iron sheets. He had noticed them lying unused in the service station. For just a few rupees, the attendant had let him have them. But he also brought back some very important information.

"I know you received a visit from Singh," the attendant had said pocketing thirty rupees, "But you didn't make a deal!"

"Not for the price he offered."

"But you still want to sell it?"

Ranji raised an eyebrow, "Are you interested now?"

"Not me. I've told you, I do not know of any likely customers, but I know he is interested. When he came to see you, he filled up with fuel at the station and he told me so. He told me he would definitely come back. I trust him because my cousin lives in Tirachpuli like him, and the Singh family has a good reputation for reliability."

"He told you that? But I thought he was from Chennai? Where is Tirachpuli?" said Ranji loading up the sheets on his back.

"About 200 kilometres from here near the border of the state."

"So it is nearer than Chennai?"

"Ah yes," the attendant said with a laugh. "Surely you didn't think he would have come all that way just to buy a tyre! Yes, he said he would come back. Be careful carrying that in this weather! You should only take one at a time."

"One! Just in case someone else wants the other one, I bet!" thought Ranji.

"Thanks for the advice," he muttered under his rickety shell as he faced the murky expanse of water on which traces of oil were tracing multi-coloured arabesques.

The sheets were heavy and bulky on his back but at least they proved effective protection. They screeched as they rubbed together under the loud claps of thunder and cut into his fingers. The sound of the rain hitting them was muffled. Bent under the load, Ranji carried his new roof and it reminded him of the feeling when he was carrying his bundles of wood. In his mind he imagined the huge improvement they would represent and how he hoped they could permanently resolve the big issue: shelter. Meena and Surya should have no need now of Ashok's compassion.

On the third day, the deluge was still building up. Ranji took advantage of a slight lull to fix the sheets with twine and he brought under shelter into the crowded hut everything they could cram in. The available living space was very much reduced.

All three of them were under the awning, watching the rain which continued to fall. They were sitting on the *charpoi* which had been raised onto four bricks because water had seeped through the join between the walls and the floor. They waited anxiously for the moment when the sky would be torn by a huge purple welt, cracked like the earth by drought, when lightning would strike a tree which stood out too prominently with a crack announcing the end of the world. And they prayed that it would not be their banyan that was struck. They would have to live like this for two months without hope of dry clothes, struggling to light a fire with sodden wood. How long could they stay under this makeshift shelter with leaks that must be patched up constantly? Ranji thought of his tyre. Had he been too stubborn in refusing any offer? But in his heart of hearts he still believed the broker would return, despite the weather.

A motorcycle stopped in front of the hut and his heart raced. The biker wrapped in an orange plastic poncho removed his helmet. It was not Mr Singh but Sharad Sarin.

"We have been expecting you for three days at the warehouse," he said, rain dripping from him. "We need all hands to consolidate the dyke!"

Ranji had thought that these conditions would have put a halt to all activity.

"Anyway you can't stay here! Has no one offered to shelter you?"

"Yes," said Ranji confused, "But I am waiting for a visit."

"Hey, come on, don't be stupid! Forget your visit, take your family somewhere dry and look to your responsibilities at work! You can't imagine that we will pay you unless you work! If you agree to go, your friend Vicash has offered to pick you all up with his cart. But you need to tell him yourself!"

He spoke then to Meena who was shivering, holding a miserable looking Surya close to her.

"You, what do you think?"

Ranji questioned his wife with a look.

"I think he's right," Meena whispered

"Come on Ranji! Get on my bike, I'll take you. Then Vicash will come back to look for them."

Rain fell like rods, wiry, powerful, taut as steel cables. This gleaming iron curtain blurred all vision. Behind this screen, there were more trees, more horizon, more landmarks. Clinging to the back of the foreman, Ranji could see nothing. A dark mist obscured and shortened distances. The day resembled dusk. They moved through this landscape which seemed as sombre and mysterious as the prayer hall of a temple. Like a huge fan, the wind distorted trees, trunks were bent like bows, the palms smacking against each other collided with a sinister creaking. But Ranji heard only the engine spitting and the swearing of Sharad. He was using his legs for balance because there was no longer a road but a river with grey waves, striated by the rain, which blurred the trucks creating phosphorescent waves.

Arriving at the brickyard, Ranji found that the hole from which the clay was extracted was filled with reddish water.

Vicash came to meet him, wading through the huge puddles dotted over the ground.

"I'm glad to see you," Ranji's friend said through the sheeting rain. "Ashok told me that his offer still stands but you must make up your mind quickly because soon there will be no room left in the warehouse. We are already a dozen families there."

"Where is he?"

"You don't need to go to see him yourself," Vicash assured his friend.

Ashok's house, with its four yellow walls advertising the cement from *Birla*, looked like an isolated island left in the world. At the side of an elongated building of mud bricks, women were scouring their dishes using the water falling from the sky. Ranji was overcome by emotion realising that soon his wife and daughter could be amongst them, dry and safe. Why had he been so stubborn!

"Right, and now we must go to the dam," said Sharad.

"I can fetch them with the cart. You only need to say the word," broke in Vicash, "It's foolish to leave them there!"

"Okay. Tell Meena to take as many things as she can. And remind her not to forget the can ..."

"So, now you see that I was right," insisted Sharad. Under his orange plastic poncho, with his helmet and glasses, he looked like a cosmonaut.

"Hurry up! We've got to go now!" he yelled.

Before getting back on the pillion of the motorcycle, Ranji took one last glance, just to check that Ashok really was not there to speak to. He had resolved that Meena and Surya must be brought to safety, but for himself, he was still determined to return to the *kheti* tonight, convinced that the broker would return to buy the tyre.

Within minutes they arrived at the lower field, where fifteen farm workers were standing knee-deep in the water. They were repairing a breach in the barrier of branches and clay that had been constructed to protect the crops. The field was sloping and the water had rushed down and built up behind it until it had eventually given way, flooding the downstream area. Some workers brought branches, others collected the muddy clay with makeshift buckets that they then poured onto the branches, in the knowledge that their efforts might not be of any use at all.

He joined forces with the others – cane cutters, cashew collectors, workers mobilized to save what they could of the remains of the lentil crop. Tirelessly they consolidated the dyke under the rain showers that started suddenly and stopped just as suddenly throughout the afternoon.

Before night fell, Ranji asked Sharad, who was coming and going between the two sites they were trying to protect, if he could go to see the barn where his cow had been put. The exasperated foreman sighed that he still had so much more important work to do that he couldn't accompany him.

"Do you know where she is?"

"Well no," answered Ranji.

"She is on the hill behind the mango orchard. It's not very close by."

"It doesn't matter. I'll go," insisted Ranji, desperate now to check on her wellbeing.

"Be careful, there is flooding everywhere. You can't miss it: it is the only building on the hill. Ask to see Ajit, he is in charge. And take a stick!"

Two hours later, when Vicash arrived with his oxen at the hut, Meena was trying to dry out Surya's homework book, smeared with violet ink, sodden and soft as a mop, over a cloud of smoke. As for Surya, she was attempting to clean her pen which had filled up with muddy water, and was shedding a quiet tear.

When Vicash explained the reason for his arrival, Meena hid her relief, but a smile illuminated her heart. Life there had become impossible. It took only a moment to gather together their few belongings, the school things in such poor condition, the precious can, all wrapped in an old turban. Meena grabbed a can of coconut oil, the stove, three glasses and a clay pot. Vicash hoisted up a bag of peas, an old tea box and the heavy water jar onto the cart and helped Meena to climb up.

"Gitika will be delighted to see you," he said to Surya.

"Are you staying there too?" she asked.

This prospect suddenly cheered up the child.

On the way, Meena was alarmed to discover the extent of the flooding. In some places the water reached the wheel hubs of the cart. One could only guess at where the road was by the trunks of trees that bordered it. The familiar landscape had changed completely: the fields had become lakes, the roads rivers, the houses islands. Approaching the brickyard, only the top of the oven was emerging like the back of a sea monster. Luckily the wooden bridge over the three ditches was well marked by barriers. Vicash found it without alarm, but after the hard ground of the road, the wheels sank deep into the clay earth and everyone crossed the last metres on foot, taking care not to fall into a quagmire.

Sheltered under a big black umbrella, Puna, Ashok's wife welcomed this bedraggled little family, with the compunction of a devotee fulfilling her duty of charity, but without smiling or touching these humble *dalit* that she would save from the water. Meena bowed many times and thanked Puna with hands clasped. Surya did the same.

Then they entered the warehouse that had been converted into a temporary dormitory. Using bags, pallets and piles of bricks, thirty people had created some semblance of privacy for themselves. The long room smelt of damp and of smoke from the fireplaces lit by each family to do their cooking. All the poor of the immediate neighbourhood were gathered together in this rudimentary building used to store the unfinished bricks. Stacked up, they formed screens, and even if one could dream of a more comfortable existence, the families were certainly better off there than in their fragile shacks. Between the piles of bricks, Gitika spotted her friend Surya and rushed over to meet her. They held hands and looked at each other smiling, happy to be reunited again.

Bahmini, Vicash's wife, suggested to Meena that she settle down near them in the corner next to the door leading to the ground floor of the house. The two women had never developed the same friendship as their husbands. Bahmini was older than Meena, a tiny woman who seemed older than her years. The misery of losing her two sons was etched permanently on a face already disfigured by smallpox. Certainly she was no beauty but she had a sweet character, focussing all her devotion on her only surviving children, little Gitika and her younger brother. She worked hard, washing the dishes in a small fast-food shop on the outskirts of Puttur, known for making a tasty biryani chicken. The two women had only met occasionally – for the Maha Shivarati festival, or at Ganesha Chaturthi – and only very rarely saw each other at the well, but Bahmini behaved just as if they were close friends. Meena unpacked her few belongings and looked for somewhere for that precious can of Pepsi which contained their money. Finding no hiding place safe enough, she decided to slip the notes into her *choli*.

CHAPTER 18
THE VISITOR

R anji had attached the tyre securely to the main trunk of the banyan. This strange tree was not chosen by chance by Buddha. With its many trunks and hanging roots that give birth to new trunks, it forms a kind of cathedral inhabited by mystery.

For three days the sky had been forbidding and sullen. Bright gaps zigzagged between the black billowy clouds. The wind dropped as suddenly as it appeared. Water flowed slowly around the hut and the collector of wood, counter of cashews, cutter of cane in the bad days, killed time, sitting on his *charpoi* looking at plastic bottles drifting past in the water.

If it could be accurately forecast from the lessening ferocity of the monsoon, they were in for a change very soon. The dyke they had built up to protect the Rajah's lentil fields so far seemed to have held. Sharad had dismissed all the workers whilst asking them to be ready to respond if he summoned them.

Stubborn in his hope that the broker would finally come back, Ranji had not joined Meena at Ashok's home and he missed his family. He told himself that if the gods were charitable, this evening before nightfall he would be able to undertake the journey, taking care not to lose his footing on the way. Under the horizontal body of water, the hidden land held many dangers, but he could count on his knowledge of the undergrowth along the roadside, so often travelled when he was collecting wood.

Suddenly, cleaving through the water like a small motor boat, a black and yellow tuk-tuk came into view. It slowed down and stopped at the roadside near the hut. For one wonderful moment, Ranji thought it was the broker! But he was disappointed. It was a woman in a white sari who, after turning up her hem and removing her sandals, placed a foot cautiously in the black water. A glance around and her gaze came to rest on the canopy under which Ranji sat, chin in his hand, a *beedi* held between his thumb and forefinger. Rather surprised, he recognized his visitor and respectfully rose to his feet.

"Hello Ranji," said the woman whose grey hair was pulled back from her face, while her thin smile hinted at an eternal sorrow.

"Hello *mam sahib*, what a surprise in this weather!"

The tragically widowed wife of *sahib* Chatterji, the flour merchant, had kept herself to herself for such a long time! The whole region had been shocked by the accident that had killed her husband and two children! Their car had collided with a wild elephant near Kottayam from where they were returning laden with cardamom, nutmeg, fenugreek and other spices. They were killed instantly.

But Ranji remembered her from happier times. It must have been two years ago that the entire village had admired her in her shining garments, riding on a horse decorated with gold, at the head of a procession of four hundred people at least. The eldest son of the Rajah, the one for whom fate had also turned out badly, had ridden directly in front of her. Ranji, who had seen the grand procession pass, remembered the orchestra of twenty-five musicians, and the joy that had emanated from this wealthy family.

Condemned so early by widowhood to live alone, to dress entirely in white, never to remarry, and marked as such by her *kum kum* of the same colour, she had remained so elegant and respected! It might have been better for her to sacrifice herself, as did the widows in former times, rather than to wither away without the chance to love again, thought Ranji.

The widow was noble, beautiful, dignified and rich, but sadness never left her face. She suppressed her grief by becoming actively involved in the school. What role did she play exactly? Ranji did not know. He knew only that she was highly respected by the teachers and that the students loved her. For Diwali, the festival of light, she had distributed amongst them thousands of lanterns, and for Holi she certainly did not hold back from sprinkling students and teachers with the ceremonial coloured powder.

"Do you know who I am? I am Aruna Chatterji," the gracious lady announced herself.

"Of course *mam sahib*! Surya often talks to me about you!"

"Is she not here? Is she OK?"

"She had to leave. She's with her mother, staying with ... a friend. Is the school still closed?"

"Yes, still closed! Even so I go there quite often, for administrative tasks and to collect the mail. So now you are staying alone in this hut?"

"That's right. In fact, I am expecting someone."

"Maybe it is me!" said the widow, with that thin smile that lit up her sad face for a moment.

Family was the most precious thing in the world to Ranji. He admired the courage of this widow in her seclusion.

He could hazard no guess at Mrs Chatterji's age, but her queenly bearing and her impeccable appearance, despite the rain and the mud, was remarkable. He noted the delicate features of her face, her fine nose embellished by a jewel rimmed with gold, the prominent cheekbones, her dark eyes subtly emphasised by kohl, her graceful attitude. The widow was not the broker as he had hoped, but her presence in that place was a blessing and her beauty was unsettling. Ranji appreciated this surprising visit.

Aruna Chatterji adjusted her umbrella and brought the little embroidered bag hanging from her shoulder round in front of her. She took out a letter.

"This was addressed to Surya, care of the school," she said, "And it comes from Thanjavur. I will entrust it to you as Surya is not here."

"From Thanjavur! This must be Santosh's reply to mine," cried Ranji, taking the letter hurriedly.

From the way he was scrutinising what was written on the envelope, the widow guessed that he could not read.

"I think I understand why he sent it to his sister. You can't read, can you?" she asked gently.

"It is true that I am not used to getting letters," explained Ranji, "But I can count well," he added, feeling the need to elaborate as he made a move to open the letter.

"But this letter is supposed to be for Surya," said Mrs Chatterji now slightly irritated.

"She is my daughter! And she is a child! I have the right to read her mail. Santosh always writes to her, because he does not know that I have made progress with my reading, thanks to Surya and to the school, so maybe a little thanks to you too! This must be from my son. It is not a problem if I open it," added Ranji, agitated and starting to unseal the envelope softened by moisture.

He extracted the single sheet and unfolded the letter covered by a cursive writing reminiscent of a field of flowers. He studied it for a moment as though reading it through but then, acknowledging to himself that he was unable to understand what was written there, he folded it again.

"If you want me to read it to you, I will willingly," offered his visitor.

Ranji smiled broadly, showing his toothless gums. The widow had offered, showing neither pride nor pity. This woman was so beautiful, and good, but widowed.

"Such a waste!" thought Ranji, looking around him for somewhere for her to sit. Everything around the *kheti* was wet. The tree trunk that served as a bench was three quarters under water. The tyre under the banyan the same. Only the string bed was a possibility, but surely it was inappropriate for an untouchable to invite a lady of her status to sit on his pitiful bed! But if he left the lady standing under her umbrella to read the letter, it would prompt her to want to leave. Maybe she would not even read it to the end. And this letter might contain the answer to the question that had tormented his mind for so many months!

"I am completely helpless, *mam sahib*, I have not even a seat to offer you! Ah, but yes, of course!"

He had just remembered that he had hung up an old cashew bag at the back of the hut and put inside it straw and dry kindling in order to light a fire. He pulled the trunk under the canopy and placed the bag on top of it to make a kind of dry cushion.

"There we are *mam sahib* Chatterji!"

The widow recognised the effort that this barefoot man had made to create for her this seat and prepared to settle down, praising his ingenuity.

"If I had sold my tyre, I would have seated you in a proper chair," he said ruefully.

"Your tyre?"

"Yes. The person I am waiting for is coming to buy it, but with the monsoon, he has been delayed."

"I wish you good luck, because you deserve it," said the widow, sitting down. Gold bracelets jingled on her wrists. From a leather case, she took out a pair of silver rimmed glasses which she placed delicately on her nose. Ranji's eyes never left her. Never had anyone of such a high status, behaving so naturally, been under the awning of his hut. The widow Chatterji, seated beside him, almost touching him, behaving like a relative or friend, began reading.

Thanjavur, 15 Sept. Aippaci

My dear little sister,

I hope you are well, and our parents too. I have been working hard because business is good, despite the rains which are disrupting the sites. We have sold many sand-bags to protect property from the water.

I have managed to save quite a lot of money. I do not know if bahba has bought the bike of his dreams yet, but as for me, I have set aside almost enough to pay for a motor-bike! (Do not tell mum). There is a very good chance that I will be able to come to see you all the next Diwali. My boss has agreed because I have not taken a single day of holiday since I started to work for him.

I am trying hard to help with bahba's tyre. My boss allows me to use his computer and I put the tyre up for sale on the internet. It's an amazing system: anyone in India and other places too, could bid for and buy the tyre. He said to me in the letter you wrote for him that he wants to make four thousand rupees, so knowing that, I proposed a price of five thousand. This is a very significant amount but you would pay much more than that in stores. Anyway we shall see! I'll keep you posted.

The monsoon is tough this year. I hope you do not have too many problems with the electricity. Here we constantly have power cuts. I am doing puja regularly and asking for protection from Bhagavati for the whole family. I can't wait to see you again. You must be growing up little sister!

I keep you close to my heart. And I send the same affection to our dear parents.

Santosh

Aruna Chatterji held the letter in her hand and clearly moved, took a little time before she turned towards Ranji. She had known the boy, lively and intelligent, and could see him in his uniform shorts, patched everywhere. And the image of her own young son snatched away by fate overlaid it. How fortune plays with human beings!

Ranji's eyes were misty. He also saw his son through the words read to him by the widow, with a mixture of pride and sadness.

"I should certainly not have read to you the part about the motorcycle!" said Mrs Chatterji mastering her melancholy, "But I'm happy for him and for you. He was a very good student!"

"Not at all, *mam sahib*, you did well to read everything! I'm so proud of my boy! He is such a worker... I do not know how to thank you."

"I remember your son very well. We put him forward to go to college. He could have continued his studies at an institute of technology, there were places reserved for..."

She was going to say *dalits* but stopped herself from stating this cruel reality check. But even so, modern India had at last begun to understand that the true worth of people has nothing to do with their caste. Positive discrimination for untouchables had already led some to the highest responsibilities in the land.

"We did not have enough money for him to continue his studies! But he has a good job now, you know. Tell me please: what is this 'internet' of which he speaks?"

"A huge communication network in India and beyond, worldwide. All you need is electricity and a computer."

"A computer?" asked Ranji, puzzled.

The widow explained with some simple words that India had taken its place among the most advanced nations in this new universe. This country which contained Ranji, the poor man in his hut of palms living below the poverty line, like more than three hundred million of his fellow countrymen, this very same country rivalled Japan and the United States in this particular area. And by the way, if he wished to, his visitor told him, he could himself go to the school, where Aruna Chatterji would show him this extraordinary machine called a computer.

"M*am sahib* Chatterji, would you mind reading to me again the part about the tyre?"

A sudden downpour. The corrugated iron sounded out like an old cracked bell, and then, battered by the rain, speech was rendered inaudible. The widow waited it out. Her upright bearing, despite her sitting on an old bag once containing nuts, commanded respect as she watched the drops ricochet on the surface of the water. Impossible to guess from her impassive face what she was feeling. Ranji suspected that behind the stillness, feelings similar to his own were struggling to show themselves. The widow was thinking we should not allow so many people to live in such misery, that Ranji was courageous, that children deserved a helping hand in their destiny.

She reread that paragraph as requested and explained to Ranji how transactions were made on the web, though that worried him greatly. How could you trust someone you couldn't see? How could you conclude a negotiation without speaking? Might it be possible that Santosh would risk buying a motorcycle that he had not seen from a stranger to whom he had not spoken?

"I'm so glad your son is succeeding in his job," she said.

She had the discretion not to ask about the origin of this tyre that seemed so important. It was Ranji who felt the need to explain the whole story and then also why he was in such haste now to receive a response via this 'internet' that his son had suggested as a solution.

"They say the results are surprising with this system," said the widow, "I'm sure you are going to sell your tyre! The gods have given you a gift, they will not let you down."

That night, the rain redoubled in its intensity. Lightning tore across the sky in all directions, for a brief moment illuminating the landscape which had been transformed into a vast pond, dotted by trees battered by the wind. Warm night fell on a desolation that had showed no mercy to the *dalit*. To try to go to Ashok's place in these conditions would have been the worst possible thing to do. He resigned himself to spending another lonely night in the hut. He thought about the widow, as he blew on the damp coal in the brazier, and pondered her story of the internet, more than a little sceptical about this strange technology. The acrid smoke swirled in the wind, stinging his eyes but at least, keeping away the mosquitoes.

In one bag, forgotten by Meena in the haste of her departure he discovered a handful of flour paste, and formed it into a patty to cook on a piece of metal, found on the road. Once cooked, he dipped it into some mango chutney and ate slowly, relishing every bite. Then, his belly hardly satisfied, he lay down on the *charpoi* praying to heaven to allow him to fall asleep despite the noise of the thunder.

The elements banded together to thwart him. He allowed his mind to dwell on the kindness of his visitor. Her positive comments had given him one of those little boosts that could enliven the routine of daily life.

Soon, however, his mind returned to wondering about the reason that could have prevented the broker from returning. The letter from Santosh opened up an obscure route that did not correspond at all to what he had been hoping for from his son. In his mind, Santosh would have spoken about his tyre to a delivery driver from Birla Cement who, in turn, would have passed on the information and without any need for the internet, this traditional chain of information would have eventually borne fruit. He was upset and would have liked to talk to his wife. He pictured Meena with Surya in Ashok's warehouse, with others as well no doubt. At least they could have discussed it if they were together.

Then his thoughts turned to Rush, his younger half-brother. They had quarrelled on the death of their mother because his brother had taken possession of the cart which the family had been given by the tuk-tuk driver when he had abandoned them. How he wished he had been able to take over the cart when Rush had left for Simla and the army.

He thought back to that time when they were both in rags. They had hustled the traders for work, offering to carry their merchandise and unload the trucks for just a few *nayé payse*. They were poor, but happy to traverse the city pushing loads as high as mountains. At that time, he got along well with this half-brother. Then everything had changed when their mother was hospitalized in the leper colony of Tenkasi. Some members of the Raoul Follereau foundation had gathered her up from the gutter and they never saw her again. Rush had laid claim to the vehicle on the pretext that it was a gift from his own father. They had fought. Rush had won.

Later that same year Rush has been accepted by the army – one of the quota of the classless – and in this way Ranji's younger soldier brother had been lucky enough to be pulled from misery, but Ranji could not forgive him for having sold the cart instead of passing it on to him. If he had owned it he would certainly then have stayed on in Chennai. His life might well have been better.

Left entirely alone, at the age Santosh was now, Ranji had taken off for the outskirts of the city, and for a time he carried cement on the construction sites. Then he moved on further West and found work as a farmhand. He married and had children, living on the edge of the city, and that was his life until that long forced journey to this little stretch of road lined with fruit trees. And he had never heard of Rush again. Maybe he was in Kashmir on one of the famous Russian trucks that drove with big tyres like his one.

Ranji did not want to think about these events that he had buried so deeply in his memory that they should never reappear, but that night, in the solitude and darkness peopled by uncertainties, they flowed back just as trash buried by time is brought to the surface by the monsoon.

It was now three days since they had left and he missed Meena and Surya terribly. They might as well have been on the borders of Ladakh, they could not have seemed further away from him. Like an inexorable ringworm, misery clung to his skin until he could be reunited with Meena. He would have given the world to her if he could, but had nothing but his affection to offer. A beautiful wife and two wonderful children had repaid him many times over with their love. This was worth more than any material wealth. And imagining Santosh able to afford a motorcycle when he himself didn't even have enough money to buy a bike, instead of making him feel low, sweetened his melancholy.

But tonight, he was alone and, fully aware of the vulnerability of his situation, he wondered how much longer he could stay there. He fell asleep curled up on the bed of strings stretched by the ever present humidity.

In the morning he woke alerted first by the smell. The hut stank of stagnant water even more so than lately. Water oozed in from all sides.

The violent wind lifted the sheets on the roof and rustled through the palms. Day did not seem to have dawned yet, but without knowing what was coming he had a foreboding of disaster. He sat up quickly, rubbed his eyes and got off the bed. It sank down, soft and sticky like the dough he had cooked the day before. All around him, Ashok's bricks were scattered, like dominoes, giving free passage to the flow of water. The whole hut trembled, driven by a titanic force that shook the structure. He understood then why he could see no signs of day: the poles supporting the canopy had collapsed and the palms were swaying and blocking the entrance. Risking a look through the interlacing greenery Ranji was rendered immobile by what he saw.

In front of him gushed, like a geyser, a torrent of disgusting water laden with mud that seemed to have been caused by some kind of obstacle. The flood was carrying entire tree trunks and all kinds of waste. His hut, miraculously spared by this tide, was still standing. The rest of the area appeared to have been destroyed by a tsunami. All around was desolation.

He carefully picked his way out of the hut and looked around him for some sign of reassurance outside. It had stopped raining but the grey haze only crystallized the nature of this place which was devoid of any signs of life. It was as if the usual crowd of pedestrians, vehicular traffic, birds and all living things had disappeared from the face of the earth.

Only the enormous banyan tree had survived – its drooping branches bent by tornadoes and the wind. Its imposing mass emerged from behind the barrier that had built up against the hut. The realisation dawned that it was this stinking pile of branches, plastic bags of all kinds and mud, diverting the waves, which had quite simply saved his life.

He approached the incredible mound that has formed overnight. No doubt a dyke or a dam must have given way upstream and he thought of the fragility of the one they had repaired in the Rajah's fields. But what god had decided to create such a barrier against the fury of the flood, exactly where it was needed to save the hut?

He had no idea, but it did not take him long to find the reason for his salvation. Inlaid in the mud, leaning against one of the protective sheets and in this way preventing it from flying off, the tyre had trapped branches, which in turn blocked all kinds of materials which built up and cemented by mud had formed an impassable wall. Everything that the water had transported in fury had piled up to protect the *kheti*.

Without the tyre, the hut would have been swept away and he with it. That's why the gods had delayed its sale! The tyre had had a crucial role to play, saving Ranji from drowning! But in performing this role, the gods had seriously compromised its sale, and that at the exact time that the hope of getting a good price was essential! It seemed that they were taunting this wretched untouchable with their own incomprehensible game...

Happy to be alive but devastated by these conditions Ranji struggled to apprehend the disaster. There must be wounded, drowned, dead. He immediately thought of his family. Would the warehouse have withstood the disaster? Given its elevated location, very likely, but Meena must be worried about him. How could he let her know that he was alive? Far too risky to venture on foot to the brickyard! And with the road buried under the floodwaters, little chance of finding transportation!

He was standing with difficulty in this strangely iridescent water that came up to his mid-thigh, wondering what he should do next, when he heard the sound of a vehicle approaching from the direction of Puttur. It was a Red Cross vehicle, headlights on, honking. This signal could be intended only for him. The Tata all-terrain truck converted into an ambulance for this eventuality, was rescuing people in distress all along the road. It came to a halt in front of the ruins of the hut and two men shod in high rubber waders exhorted Ranji to climb up into the back.

A dozen people were sitting on the bench, blankets over their heads, looking haggard and shivering despite the heat. He recognized Doria, the beggar from near the temple, but he was alone, and seeing the tears dripping down his face Ranji was reluctant to dwell on the reason. He realized then that he too was trembling head to toe. The closest man on the bench turned to him, handing him a khaki plaid army blanket. It was the obliging attendant from Indian Oil.

"The sheets were not enough..." he said, looking at the shapeless mass which had been Ranji's home. "Sorry..."

The man had picked up the thirty rupees with just his fingertips, reluctant to touch those of Ranji, who remembered the slight well. Now he was right up against him and no longer feared that contact. With head covered and tossed about by the bumps on the journey he was in exactly the same boat as the *dalit*. His hands glistening with oil, and covered with scratches, he described his battle when the fuel tank was pushed up by the flood waters. Pipes came loose, the fuel was dispersed on the surface of the water and he feared that as well as the disaster of the flood, there was now a serious risk of fire. Ranji realised that it was his petrol that had traced these multi-coloured swirls on the water that resembled the wings of dragonflies! Relieved to have shared the story of his struggle with someone, the man added:

"So anyway, you saw Singh?"

"Well no. I waited, and I was still waiting yesterday…"

"He called me on the phone just before the storm. He was going to return one of these days. I think he had a new offer for you."

They were gathered together in the centre of the village of Puttur, in an indescribable confusion, everything that could be saved, humans, animals and vehicles. Crowds of victims were huddled in the courtyard of the *panshayat*, the place spared from the floods by the wisdom of the ancient people who had established it at the highest point of the village. Some women seemed about to faint, others were hysterically screaming or bemoaning their misfortune, as if the calamity had affected them alone. The drivers of *tuk-tuks* were camped out on the roofs of their vehicles. Meanwhile children were playing amid the mud, unconscious of the drama around them. Men congregated around those in uniform, pleading that the fire engine coming from Puttur should make it their absolute priority to extract water from their houses in the lower village. Bank notes were slipped into hands by some trying to advance up the queue for help more quickly.

Some cursed, others fretted to themselves faced with this indescribable mess. Announced in advance by their loud horns, the Red Cross vehicles brought in more and more refugees, even though the courtyard was already completely full. Peasants in a state of shock arrived with their families. Vagabonds and the well-to-do found themselves side by side, each as poor as the other. They railed against the administration, incapable officials, the disorganization of the rescue effort, the corruption of politicians who had done nothing to prevent this disaster despite their outlandish projects. If it hadn't been for the presence of those anonymous dead whose bodies, covered by a blanket, were lined up along the walls, and the defeated faces of those who came to check if they could find one of their own, it could have been one of those devotional or political assemblies that punctuated the course of the year.

The loudspeaker repeated hygiene instructions on a loop: do not drink water from the well, cook all foods, don't light a fire, keep calm. The injured should wait where they were for medical aid to arrive. The authorities were trying to take care of everything and everyone, yet everyone was trying to look out for themselves among the multitude, so no one listened to the voice of reason and the chaos grew worse.

Ranji wandered for a long time in the midst of this helpless crowd. He would have appreciated being able to put one of those cell phones brandished by the wealthy amongst them to his own ear! As they spoke loudly he could hear the reassurances of those close by, and he heard their enquiries about the situation elsewhere. He had had no news of the brickyard. No-one could put his mind at rest. He passed some inert bodies which a medical team were examining. A nurse covered those found dead with a blanket, leaving their faces uncovered to aid identification.

And that is where Ranji came across him, with his white shirt collar stained with blood and mud, his neat beard dotted with tiny thorns. They had picked up Mr Singh near the village, on the road to Puttur, stuck like a straw in the tangled bushes, twenty metres away from his Honda motorcycle.

Ranji's eyes no longer obeyed him. He fell to the ground and remained there prostrate, his face buried in his dirty hands, and he began to weep. And the more he cried the more he felt the utter despair of having lost his most promising hope. The broker had died coming to buy his tyre!

The tears froze on his face with the arrival of reinforcements from the army. Five trucks carrying soldiers and pumps, bags of rice and generators caused a stampede. A Russian truck converted into a mobile hospital particularly caught his attention. His eyes sized up the tyres, and he recognised the make, emphasised by the mud, those letters engraved in his memory.

Exactly the same as his own!

And thinking about the state in which he had left it, he buried his face in his hands, crushed by this terrible disappointment.

Chapter 19
New Horizons, New Hope

In a material way, Ashok was certainly well placed. His house had a real terrace and a second floor. But no-one could ever describe it as stylish. A large cube pierced with rectangular holes barred with thin iron rods, it was grimly reminiscent of a prison building. The entire facade facing the road was painted yellow, and large blue letters extolled the merits of *Birla* cement, who had paid for this distemper job. On the wall that faced the adjoining warehouse and the Rajah's fields the bricks produced by the owner could be seen under a smear of plaster.

Ashok and his family lived upstairs. The ground floor, where their servants lived, was connected by a door to the warehouse so it was accessible without having to go outside. The space granted to Meena and Surya was near this door, not far from the place where Vicash and his family were, all of them camped amongst shovels, stores and piles of bricks. The children adapted quickly to this closeness and companionship which reminded them of being at school. Their active imaginations and the freedom to explore the warehouse meant they passed the time happily. The refugees couldn't do other than bless him who had kept them dry, even if they knew that one day they would be made to pay in one way or another for his kindness.

During the evening of that terrible night that would devastate the area, water had begun to seep through the dirt floor. The men repositioned the sandbags stored in the room to try to stop the encroaching moisture. Given the impossibility of sleeping directly on the damp ground, everyone had their own innovations. Bricks were unloaded from the pallets, and they were converted into uncomfortable benches. Vicash helped Meena to make a platform next to their own, but even so she hardly closed her eyes all night.

She lay awake plagued by worry and speculation, wondering if Ranji had been able to leave the hut and where he could be. Clutching her daughter tight against her, despite the muggy heat, she fought against the crazy thoughts jostling in her mind that stopped her from falling asleep. The snoring of the men was punctuated by the roar of thunder, and the water rattled on the roof in waves.

The feeling of being on a sinking ship on a lake increased her torment. She imagined the water accumulating around them and their hut buried beneath the flood. Sometimes the crying of a child awakened those who slept and their grunts were heard above the din of the elements. Meena was jolted awake, startled. Surya stirred, yawned and went back to sleep, indifferent to her surroundings. Were there enough sheets on the roof to hold back the raging elements? The courage and perseverance of her man suddenly appeared to her as priceless virtues. And she prayed with all her heart that his hopes would be rewarded! How she wished for the return of the broker! But would he have come in this weather?

And how she regretted her frivolity, her vague pleasure, her ambiguous thoughts inspired by Ashok's courtship, this man to whom she owed so much and who was sleeping soundly, not far from her, maybe even dreaming about her. The consciousness of her weakness tore at her heart like the lightning across the heavens. She was searching for a way to beg for the mercy of the gods in a more perfect way than ever before, making promises, resolutions …if they would only keep her husband safe. Were they punishing her with this heartbreak for the pleasure she had experienced in feeling desired?

The demons have fun tormenting women. So when the door opened and she saw the face of the one that she felt herself cursed to find attractive, with his shiny hair and domineering manner, she buried her face hastily in her veil and pretended to be deeply asleep. Summoning every ounce of her resolve to swear that she would never ever give herself to this demon.

But Ashok had come only to announce that the new day had dawned. Raising his voice, he said there had been terrible flooding and there was much damage. To Meena who was struggling to regain her composure, he said with a big smile that her husband had been rescued unharmed, and had found shelter in the village.

"I hope now that he will accept my hospitality," he added sincerely.

Meena spontaneously joined her hands and bowed to Ashok.

"Thank you Ashok *sahib*, thank you for everything," she said in a whisper barely audible, because already the news had caused a loud commotion in the room. "We must go immediately to join him."

"Oh no! It is he who must come here. Vicash is just about to leave to go looking for him."

Meena turned towards the next pallet. Ranji's friend was no longer there. His wife nodded at the words of Ashok.

The gods had taken up more water than usual from the Indian Ocean that year and the sky evacuated its burden by pouring massive amounts on Kerala and Tamil Nadu. Once the fury of the gods had been appeased, the clouds vanished into the ether, farmers returned to the fields, truckers to their vehicles, officials to their offices. After having caused so much trouble, the flood had also brought with it deposits of silt that were very good for the soil. The roadsides, cleansed by the water of huge amounts of trash, had never been so clean. The mounds of waste left behind became a gold mine for the poor who had lost their homes. Metal collectors, plastic collectors, recyclers of all kinds would be kept busy for days. Fate snatches away and gives back as it wishes, provided you know how to adapt.

Beset by negative thoughts, Ranji dozed fitfully, the death of Singh having at a stroke eliminated any real prospect of ever selling his tyre. The broker on whom fate seemed to smile had lost his life, while he, seemingly designated a victim, was unhurt. A succession of good luck and then misfortune: such was his karma. To complain in those conditions would have been unworthy of a good Hindu. It was a safe bet that his hut would have been swept away by now by the floodwaters. He understood that this catastrophe must usher in a new start. If Meena had not taken care of the Pepsi can, they would have nothing with which to restart.

Ranji became increasingly impatient and when there was a lull in the downpour he decided he could wait for news no longer. He set off from the village intending to walk to the brickmaker's house, and was joined by two other victims of the flood who were desperate to assess the damage to their homes. Armed with sticks to probe the ground in front of them, the three followed the road. It was easy enough to keep close to the trunks which had been labelled by the men from the administration on that fateful day that had deprived him of his livelihood.

They walked for a long time through a landscape that was now unrecognisable. In the fields which were now shining ponds, flamingos were seeking food. All those beaks and necks created beautiful shapes reflected in the water. Colonies of white herons occupied the space left by crows. Here and there, the landscape bore the marks of the recent erosion; projections of partially unearthed rocks, water corridors created by the overflowing ditches, these all altered the appearance of the road that had been so familiar to them.

In the far distance Ranji saw Ashok's house perched on the hillock overlooking the brickyard. Before the flood, thick bushes had hidden the house from the road. Now it looked like a fort surveying the winding of a lake that had no end in sight. With a shock he recognized the banyan tree, with its characteristic silhouette and the ten trunks diving into the water. Nothing remained around it except a vague mound. Was it possible that this was all that was left of his hut?

The closer he came to it the clearer this became: the storm had destroyed his hut and transformed it into a shapeless heap, a reef in the middle of a lake. Sick at heart, Ranji went towards it, where so many memories now lay drowned. He did not even bother to stop there. One desire alone was driving his progress now: to see his family as soon as he possibly could.

When they arrived at the upper part of the sloping field, people the colour of the earth were busying themselves around a pump, making the clay soil reappear. A semblance of life was coming back into the countryside.

A truck loaded with bales of hay passed by slowly. The ripples from its wake splashed up over his legs and wet the edge of his *dohti*. Then a yoked cart appeared ahead of him on the road. It took Ranji some time before he could identify the colour of the horns. He was sure he recognized the oxen of Vicash. Overtaking a line of people, and planting his stick in front of him to avoid falling into a hole, he quickened his pace. Two people were seated on the bench beside Vicash. His heart gave a giant leap.

Suppressing the urge to run to meet them, he lengthened his steps, drawing new energy from his happiness at finding them. Sitting up on the bench, Surya was looking directly at him but she was not yet sure that it was her father. When she was certain that it was him who was wading through the water with his stick, she waved her arms madly in all directions and he answered in the same way.

In his haste, Ranji forgot caution and fell. He tried to get up but his legs couldn't get a grip in the soft brown paste, similar to jelly, and he remained stuck where he was. The current was pushing him away from the road into the ditch alongside. Gesticulating like a devil, he managed to keep his head above water. He felt something light brush against him, turned in alarm, and brushed away the plastic bag that had scared him. He finally gained purchase on firmer ground, and managed to get to his feet, but he had lost his stick.

He could do nothing but wait where he was. When the line of walkers caught up with him they invited him to follow them, but he explained that he had reached his goal. And moments later, he was pulled out by Meena who hugged him against her. "My Ranji, you're alive!" was the only sentence she could produce.

"You know, I have had time to think," said Ranji.

All three of them were sitting on a pallet in Ashok's warehouse, each holding a small jug of steaming tea, a blanket over their shoulders. Ranji had recounted his odyssey. How he had miraculously escaped the destruction of the *kheti*, his gruesome discovery of the broker in the village, and the crossing of the utter desolation to come to find them.

"Everything happens for a reason. The tyre saved my life. I don't even know what has become of it. Maybe the water has taken it away to another poor man. Or maybe it has stayed behind in the rubble that protected the hut when it saved me. If it is still there, I will not sell it. I'm too much in its debt for protecting me."

Meena nodded her head.

"You present things with your own interpretation," she said, though without any rancour. "If the tyre hadn't fallen from the truck, you wouldn't have had to stay behind to sell it. The broker wouldn't have come. So you wouldn't have had to wait and you would have been asleep under shelter rather than risking your life in the hut…"

"But you are forgetting things that are much more important, Meena. Because of this tyre, I was hired by the Rajah. I improved my education, and I came to understand that, sooner or later, perseverance is always rewarded. If it hadn't been for this terrible flood, I would have sold it, and probably for a very good price. We cannot fight fate! Certainly, we will need courage to rebuild the hut, but if the gods have decided to keep us safe and together, it is because they trust in us."

"I noticed a lot of things as I walked along the road," Ranji continued. "The flood carried with it many things, but above all the material that is needed here at Ashok's. This material, which held my feet fast, and prevented me from running to join you, is actually very valuable. It can bring wealth ... it did so for Ashok, it could well for us too now that it covers the road. There is clay, for free!"

He went on: "As for Ashok, he has shown he is a good Hindu by looking after you in his house. He is not as bad as I thought. I think I have an idea that may interest him."

EPILOGUE

A white minibus stops on the road to Radapakkam. Ten European tourists disembark eager to discover traditional India. Not that of Bangalore, with its glass buildings and ultramodern industrial complexes, not that of the mobile phones and laptops, but the picturesque India with flaming gods and topless goddesses, pink granite temples and poor smiling children. This country of a thousand faces that abandons the poor to their dreams of riches in a future life, and allows the rich immediate international recognition. Floppy hats on their heads, cameras in hand, armed with digital devices of all kinds, they stop to take in the life of another era that unfolds along the edges of these bitumen roads. Jawarlal, their guide, in gold-rimmed sunglasses and crisp white shirt, gives them some explanation in his broken French learned at the French Alliance:

"Madam, sir, we'll stop here, under this banyan – its real name is "banyan fig tree" – a tree that has the characteristic to multiply its trunks with dangling roots. You can see next to it a small oven and a potter in his work. The lady is very nice, she grills cashews and you can buy them for a few rupees. Be careful crossing the road!"

Some earthenware jars for flour, roughly a *marakkal*, the size dictated by the small dimension of the oven, are drying out in the sun. Next to his rudimentary shelter covered with palms, an ageless man, with rolled-up *vesti*, crouches in front of it. This routine is now very familiar to him. He waits until the tourists are all gathered around him before starting his demonstration.

He places the ball of red clay on the cement which serves as a turning plate and pushes with both hands the thick disk outlined by black rubber. His oddly positioned leg takes over from his hands and his foot applies an alternating pressure on the edge of the spinning thing which happens to be the tread of a very large tyre.

Everyone raves about the ingenuity of the system: by acting as a flywheel, the cement poured into this perfectly circular mould gives mass to the rotation. No need for complicated gears, simply the pressure of his foot on the grooved surface of the tyre is sufficient to generate a regular movement.

Ranji then plunges his wet hands into the centre of the clay and the ball rises gradually under the guidance of this ancient combination of clay, hand and rotation. It doesn't take long for a pot to be produced under his expert hand.

A few rupees given to thank him and the potter finishes his work. Everyone gets back on the bus, happy to have entered into this scene, but none can imagine the emotional bond that binds the man to his wheel or could suspect that this tyre has never driven on any road. Let alone imagine the events that led this man from picking spice to his conversion into a potter.

The idea came to him after the disaster of the monsoon. Once the waters withdrew to the river, a thin layer of clay was left behind on the road. All that remained of the *kheti*

was a shapeless mass of palms and various ruined items, but the corrugated sheets were still there and the tyre, though ruined, had filled up with this fine soft clay. The trench all around was filled with alluvium which proved rich in nutritious matter and green grass soon began to grow there. The cow came back in better shape than she had been in when she went away and she revelled in these new green shoots. Ranji buckled down and decided to rebuild a stronger hut using what the flood waters had caused to become available: a lot of driftwood and clay!

The discovery, as opportune as that which had launched Meena in the roasting of cashews, paved the way for the collection of this free material which, ironically, came principally from the brickyard. Ranji decided to build an oven, taking care not to encroach on the road or on the neighbouring land. He had no intention of competing with Ashok, but having observed his oven, he had no difficulty in achieving a simple but much smaller copy.

The kindness of one of Ashok's workers allowed him to learn the basics. He became a potter as he had done everything else, through observation and experimentation. So, when Sharad Sarin asked him to resume work in the service of the Rajah, he refused but with all appropriate form, and offered him one of his first clay dishes as a thank you.

The transformation of the tyre into a potter's wheel gave a definitive meaning to the event that had brought him such an improbable cargo, on that far off day. Converted to potting and approaching it with the same seriousness he brought to all his previous activities, Ranji tried manufacturing larger containers but then became a specialist in a specific size: the *marakkal*.

Ashok had succeeded in gaining for himself nothing but trouble, and Meena was in the same situation. In this game of seduction, though feeding inaccessible dreams, neither one nor the other had taken the final step. Old Celamna, the midwife and expert on potions and magic, consulted by Meena, had prepared for her a mixture of the type designed to fight confusion of the senses. A potion of chaste berry tree taken daily would calm the libido which so much disturbed her. While she prepared the potion, Celamna chanted through her teeth, reddened by betel, esoteric formulas addressed to the womaniser.

It took effect very quickly, unless it was the test of the monsoon which, sweeping aside all former certainties, touched the heart of the seducer by revealing the courage of Ranji, and the loyalty of Meena. The gods were truly watching over this family, and eventually respect won out over desire, because in reality, the pariah, the good-for-nothing, spice-collector, wood-gatherer, cane-cutter, rebuilder-of-dams, proved himself worthy of her after all. Relations between Ranji and Ashok evolved from contempt to a strange kind of working brotherhood cemented by clay. They even managed to laugh about their former animosity.

No one ever knew for sure what had prompted the broker to return to the village despite the weather forecast. His body was burned along with eleven other flood victims. His ashes, scattered in the Cauvery river, took the mystery with them. Ranji, who attended the ceremony, did not dare to question the brothers of the deceased but he remained convinced that he had returned to buy his tyre. Meena always thought the reason was something else.

Surya was chosen as the most deserving student of Class Eight, and benefitted from the assistance plan for the education of girls from families living below the poverty line. Having spent most of her free time outdoors, looking up at the sky and the white marks traced there by aeroplanes, she decided that one day she too would fly up there above the birds. She wanted to become a pilot and follow in the path opened up by the Indian astronaut Kalpana Chawla – the one who was so tragically lost in the explosion of the shuttle Columbia.

A lovely girl, with a face that reminded one of the beautiful movie actress Madhuri Bhattacharya, in the future Ranji would receive many marriage proposals for Surya from upper castes, something he had never imagined. But Ranji rejected them all. The potter who had once dared to say "No!" had a new found pride, and was confident in the destiny of his daughter.

Dressed in smart new clothes, on his blue Japanese motorcycle, Santosh arrived two days before *Karthigai Deepam*, the Festival of Lights following the terrible monsoon. After more than a year's absence, the return of their son to light the lamps brought inexpressible joy to Meena and Ranji. He had matured so much since leaving that, when he lifted up the visor of his helmet, they had barely recognised him as the young boy who had waved to them from the bus, a nervous smile on his lips. The Festival of Lights took on a special meaning with the illumination of the platform that preceded the building of a new *kheti*. The flames of a hundred small containers made by Ranji lit up the base of bricks. With its roof of woven palms and corrugated sheets, battered but geometric, the new hut looked something like a garden shed.

Santosh had not come back empty-handed. Four one hundred rupee notes were added to the first profits that had come from the earthenware pots, and the next day Ranji exchanged these carefully collected savings for a bicycle, a Royal Enfield, second-hand, but in good condition, with a dynamo light and luggage rack. Pedalling furiously on this bike, he followed in the wake of Santosh's blue motorbike, as he rode to the temple of Vishnu, with Meena clinging tightly to her son's waist while Surya rode side-saddle on the fuel tank.

Leaning now against a pole of the hut, this black bicycle, similar to so many others, would have had a good tale to tell tourists of the adventures which had brought it there. It could have spoken eloquently of the hardships endured by its owner, and its connection with the large tyre loaded with clay which surprised them so much, but it is a well-known fact that bicycles, like old potters, are modest and prefer to protect their privacy with silence.

Lightning Source UK Ltd.
Milton Keynes UK
UKHW01f2349040918
328354UK00001B/113/P